THE
ANCIENT
SACRED TREE

BIRTHING A HERO

Dawnette N. Brenner

PAGE PUBLISHING, INC.
New York, NY

First originally published by Page Publishing, Inc. 2017

ISBN 978-1-64027-289-7 (Paperback)
ISBN 978-1-64027-290-3 (Digital)

Printed in the United States of America

THE ANCIENT SACRED TREE: BIRTHING A HERO

This story is no ordinary tale, and it is about an extraordinary boy who thought of himself as a lost soul. The events in this story are about his boyish adventures toward self-discovery and the inward confidence given him by his status in the alternate world. It is through this journey into his imagination that he is able to self-soothe in earthly form and become not only a king of the alternate world, but the leader of many suffering the same disorder. This is a fictional story written about the mind of a nonfictional child.

CHAPTER

I was real young. I didn't know what was going on. I knew Dad was missing, but I didn't know why.

—Anonymous eight-year-old girl

I'm not sure why, but my insides were swollen. I felt like they were going to just explode at any moment. My head was throbbing excruciatingly, and I felt like nobody cared about me.

Last night, I received the worst news that a child could ever hear: *My mother and father were getting a divorce!* I'm not sure what I did, but I know it's my fault. I have problems controlling my emotions, and well, I guess that made them mad at each other. So what was I to do about it? Mom said she couldn't live with Dad anymore, and well, my dad wasn't really sure what hit him. So it must be me, right? How would you react if your parents were divorcing for no good reason?

Joshua Creed, that's me, the youngest of my four siblings. The one who, most of the time, noticed my parents' arguments. Recently, my mother and father had been arguing a lot, and to deal with my anger, I usually always climbed into the world of my imagination. Other worlds, those inside *my* mind, didn't have such problems. The people merely battled for their survival. Usually, there was a villain, and I was the hero. In the real world, my brother and sisters cared about me, but you wouldn't know it by watching them. My big brother, Jonah, bossed me around and laughed at everything I did, and my biggest sister, Jada, never let me get near her, let alone hug her. Leilani was closer to my own age of eight and usually the only one to play with me. She was also a bit bossy, and we had a love-hate relationship.

"Hey, what's the big idea?" I yelled as Leilani toppled on top of my bed.

"Did you forget that we have play practice today? You have to get there early to help Mr. Ed put together the set before school," said my nine-year-old sister.

"Okay, but get out of here! You didn't even knock, and I hate it when you just barge into my room!" I yelled. "Mom, she's in my room again!"

My brother and sisters were always bothering me. I don't think they like me very much. Nobody liked me.

"Josh, I sent her in to tell you we have to go! Come on, you're always dawdling in the morning. Get the lead out, and march down these stairs right now," said my mom.

"I'm coming, but tell Leilani to stay out of my room," I said, annoyed.

Mom called Leilani to talk to her. I hoped she really got it. I hated my life. I was so frustrated. I just wished everyone would leave me alone!

I grabbed my warm cinnamon-flavored oatmeal off the table and gobbled it down, put my blue Spiderman backpack on my shoulders, and prepared to dash outside. Mom yelled something about my jacket and me not brushing my hair, but I didn't respond. I kicked open the door and slammed it shut and ran off to school! I don't need a stupid jacket; they make me sweat.

I lived really close to school and heard the warning bell, the last bell of the morning, as some kids rushed along with their parents and I exited the pebbled pathway that led from our house to the sidewalk. The morning air was damp and cool, the sun too low for warmth, as I headed to school. I only walk to school on days my mom works.

Usually my big brother walks with me, but today he overslept. Mom never gets mad at him, and I can't see why she lets him do whatever he wants. Nobody else gets the attention he does. He always gets to stay home when he's been up too late or when he forgets to do his homework. Music is his life and the reason I didn't get much sleep last night.

"Mi, mi, mi, ooh, ooh ooh, aww, aww, aww" all night long. He sings too loud and doesn't care about the rest of us, at least that's how I feel. My brother sings in five choirs, and nothing else matters to him, especially not me! So off I walked, by myself, which is how I spend most of my life—alone! I hate my life!

I heard birds singing from everywhere as I looked in every direction except directly in front of me. I saw a couple walking down the street arguing, and I thought of my mom and dad. The morning was fogged over by the sad news of my parents divorcing! I thought to myself, *Damn, why do they have to divorce now?* And after twelve years of marriage, they were heading to divorce court. Deep in thought and in my own little world, I failed to see the stroller heading my way.

"Ugh, oh, ouch!" I said as it ran over my toe and I started to hop on one foot. I felt my other foot slip, and my body toppled over, but there was nothing I could do because it happened so fast and nothing could stop me from falling. Thud! I hit the ground hard, and everything went black.

CHAPTER

Divorce is like two lions in a den attacking each other. You know somebody is going to get hurt real bad. All kids can do is sit behind a window and watch it happen.

—Anonymous nine-year-old boy

L ater that morning, I woke up to an unfamiliar sound, like that of ice cracking and images of long green blades that looked like slippery slides, due to the wetness, frost, and their shape. I could see my breath separating from my mouth as I breathed.

Oh, I'm so cold…I guess I should have listened to Mom and brought my jacket. W-w-what is this place? Where am I? As I got up, I felt kind of dizzy and had to balance myself as I stood up. "Whoah." Lightheaded, I looked around.

I'd never seen anything like this before. Smells of dampness filled my nostrils as I breathed, dew drops glistened everywhere, covering the greenery and flowers. They clung to the air as I inhaled, which reminded me of foggy days at my grandma's old house on the island. I realized I was surrounded by giant slides everywhere—like an adventure playground ten times the size of my own backyard. The ground was covered in a brownish carpet, like dirt, and every so often, I could see purplish flowers where the sun burst into this place. Dazed and confused, I attempted to figure out where I was, when all of a sudden, something brushed my shoulder. I yelled out, "What the heck?"

"Hello and welcome to the world of the Ice Plants," said a worm.

A worm? Did I just say that? Is it possible? A life-size worm? Okay, maybe this whole place is a dream. I opened and closed my eyes again. Yep, it's still a fat, bright-yellow worm, one with a tall hat and a bronze-colored trinket around its neck. It began to talk again.

"My name is Wormly. I'm the leader of the *Ice Plants* and have come to welcome you to our world. You don't really look like anyone from around here. I suspect you are the one sent here to help us. By the way, you've crushed my house," Wormly said with sad expression.

Just then I fell over again and sat on what appeared to be a rock. Checking everything out around me, I reacted. My body began to shake. I turned on my heels and peered in all directions. I felt both a sense of panic and a rush of excitement.

Where am I? How did I get down here? I could still hear the school bell ring as I sped up and rushed to school. When everything went black. *I vaguely remember being hit by some enormous stroller. Oh, my head hurts, and I really need to talk to Mom. She'll be so worried. I wonder how long I've been here. Maybe I'm dreaming …yeah…dreaming. I'll pinch myself and wake from this freakish happening.* At the same time, I realized the worm was still there.

"Hello," said Wormly, his voice echoed, finally trailing off down a passageway behind me. "Anyone home in there?" he said. "I say again, I've come to welcome you." He slithered along next to me as if we were best buddies about to engage in a serious chum session and tapped on my head.

I tried to pinch myself awake, but before I could determine whether or not I was asleep and ascertain whether I could even feel the pinch, I felt the tap on my head.

"Stop it—stop doing that. It hurts. W-w-w-h-at? Who are you? What is this place? Are you real? Where am I?" I asked, demanding answers.

"You, my good friend, are in the Land of the Ice Plants and Norkels. You've been summoned by me to help us fight the evil Thragons."

"The what?" I said as I scratched my head.

"Thragons. You have to help us," Wormly said, tilting his head to the side.

"Who, me? You expect me, me? Me, to fight?" I asked.

"Yes. Thragons are destructive, gargoyle-like creatures that hone in on their victims, toying with them like lions do with their prey before dragging them to the king," Wormly said.

"Uh, who in the world would want to encounter someone like that? I know I don't," I said, stepping backward.

"That's exactly why we need your help. You see Gonthragon is their king, a bat-like winged creature. He wreaks, spats, and breathes fire and gives evil a new name. He's long known for a promise and prophecy told for years, one in which he's caused destruction to our world," said Wormly.

"A prophecy? One that includes me? But I don't under-stand," I said, not really wanting to know the answer.

"One that includes you, yes," responded Wormly.

"Yikes, don't want to run into him. Can a prophecy be changed?" I asked.

"I don't know. For a month or so, we have taken the hit badly. Doomsday and destruction awaits us, if we don't tell him the secret of our slippery slides," Wormly said, half-happy, but seemingly worried about something.

"And…what exactly does that have to do with me?" I questioned with my hands now at my sides as I stood slouched with my neck arched looking at him.

"Look around, do you notice the over population of the huge thick green blades surrounded by purple flowers?" Wormly gestured by roaming around and glancing back toward me over his shoulder.

"These are called slippery slides, since they are always wet with dew and we tend to slide around on them and get around on them sometimes. Yet their true purpose is contained within the elixir inside the blades that have powers and Gonthragon has sworn to claim it his way, if we don't provide it to him," he said looking toward me again.

Wormly continued, "Gonthragon resides in the grasslands. He has already destroyed several acres of our land and weakened the Norkels for months now. He's turned several of our kind into Thragon's and set several regions on fire. The end is near. Through harnessed focus and severe concentration last night, I wished for a miracle. The spirits heard me. This morning *you* crushed my house! Whilst most people would likely have been angry, I was elated because I knew *your* presence brought hope to save our kind. Please help us! You have to save our people," begged Wormly.

"Uh, well, what can I do? I'm only eight and I'm not very good at anything. I'm not sure I'll be much help," I said, got up, shrugged my shoulders and looked at Wormly.

"You are destined to save us and although you may not know this, your spirit within is surging with a tremendous energy and courage, which we need," Wormly said.

Energy, what does he mean? I'm lazy. My mom says that all the time. I need to get back to mom. I cannot help fight this Gonthragon.

"Wormly is it? My name is Joshua Creed and although I feel sorry for you, I'm afraid I will be of no use to you. But please tell me, how exactly did I get here and how are you going to send me back?" I questioned, standing tall and being direct.

"I summoned the spirits to bring you here. So you can't just leave. Please say you'll join us, we'll perish without your help," Wormly begged.

Astonished, all I can do is listen. Nobody has ever needed MY help.

"During my meditation last night after sunset, I asked the spirits to send someone to us. While waiting for guidance this morning, I sought my acquaintances to help. They will arrive soon pending my signal and your decision," Wormly said kindly, but with desperation in his tone.

For a moment I looked down at the source of my pain from earlier today, the wound on the end of my toe. I realized that I felt extremely relaxed here. No worries, no pains, and no headaches. My stomach felt normal too. I thought and asked myself, *when was the last time I felt this way?* I felt as though I could spill out all over the place and not get into trouble. Wow, what a rush!

"I know my family won't really miss me, but I love my mom and want to make her proud of me—uh, someday, and if I'm stuck in this place that will never happen. So how can I get home?" I asked my new friend and ignored his plea.

"Well, we have been overpowered by the Thragons for quite some time. We don't understand it, but they have some type of power to control us, weakening our strength to fight. We absolutely buckle when it comes time to battle, due to their power over our strength and if you can help us, perhaps we can defeat them once and for all and that's the only way to get you permanently home," exclaimed Wormly.

"Dang, well, you and I are both in trouble. I cannot help with anything having to do with emotions. I have trouble containing my emotions in *my* own world. How can I offer my services? Honestly, I don't really feel like myself right now and am not convinced I'm the one to help you. I'm not a leader. I can't even lead myself out of trouble."

Meanwhile reality had taken hold of my mind and I thought about the day and how I felt. Past events taught me that I don't do well under pressure, especially in highly anxious situations. But my usual feelings of anger and outrage were gone in this of the Ice Plants! I felt, well, almost *"normal,"* like a weight had been lifted from my shoulders, but I didn't know why. An energy like nothing I'd ever felt before had taken over my body and I felt invincible. Sort of like the times I escaped my own life at home in my backyard in an imaginary world with no limits and endless opportunities to express myself. Perhaps I could just wander off and explore this land to discover what it is that was making me feel this way.

I spun on my heels and began to walk around. Blades of green grass twenty-five times larger than me glistened in the darkness of the space I occupied. For a time I poked and prodded, which caused purple flowers to open and close and large yellow bugs crawled over the grass and sought shelter. I shuffled my feet across the ground, dirt flew into the air in clouds of dust. My Carelessness caused me to trip and I slid through an opening twisted around to the other side of the room on one of the slides.

"Woohoo!" I yelled.

I just couldn't keep my hands to myself! The atmosphere was dark and cold. The roof was a vast array of the slides I encountered and seemed to go on endlessly. Sunshine peeked through sparingly and flowers, randomly spaced, appeared to open and close with the slightest of motion, as I passed by. I grew more curious and thought of what Wormly had said.

"Hey, you mentioned spirits, what are those?" I asked.

"The spirits of the Ancient Sacred Tree are rumored to connect to our spirits and they help us out when needed. They keep things in our world in balance. Without them we cannot thrive," said Wormly.

"I'd like to learn more about those spirits. I could use some balance myself. But do you mind if I explore a little?

Perhaps I'll be better prepared to help you if I know more about this place," I said as my eyes began to roam around before I got an answer.

"Sure, but you'll need a guide. I don't want you traveling around these parts blindly. You might run into a trap or worse yet, Thragons," said Wormly.

I sighed at the thought of having company on my adventure. I usually explored new places on my own. I entered *my* imaginary worlds all on my own, battled the evil villains, and still was able to come home in time for dinner. Well, at home and in my backyard was the *usual* place for my adventures. This was a new world and having a companion would put a damper on my plan, I suspected, but I was willing to give it a go. As wonderful of a place it seemed to be, I really didn't want to get trapped.

"Attention everyone," Wormly spoke and all at once, I was surrounded by the inhabitants of this cold region, all eyes on me.

Thousands of creatures assembled around me. Those closest to me could be described as purple-legged, short, almost humanlike, yellow-skinned creatures with large heads and oval protruding eyes penetrated my own eyes. Large ants, the size of large dogs, were also in the crowd. Between them were a few other wormlike creatures, perhaps Wormly's kin?

"Please take notice, Joshua Creed, our warrior of truth, has made his journey to our land and it is our obligation to grant his every wish, fulfilling his needs will help him sustain longevity and uplift his spirits to help our people. We need his help to defeat the Thragons," he proclaimed to the crowd.

He turned to me, "My friend, I would like to introduce to you, the one and only, Soran. He seeks adventure around every twist and turn of our regions, but does so with safety in mind."

My eyes twisted and enlarged a bit at the site of him. Something about him seemed a bit familiar. Had I met him before? Strange.

Wormly addressed the crowd in a loud, commanding voice. "He is our spiritual healer and helps those who've lost their way, he's a bit of a risk-taker and enjoys adventures. He will guide you on your journeys and explorations. If you need anything from me, just let him know and he'll summon some-one to get me. Now I trust you are ready?" Wormly said, as he puffed out his chest.

"Uh, well...yes, I guess I'm ready! I think...," I said, half-convinced.

"Do you desire anything further before you leave?" Wormly asked.

I gazed at my new guide and examined him through *my special eyes,* which for some reason, as I've long been told, helped me *see* things most people cannot. I'm special in this way. I'm a bit of a fortune-teller, but I've never told a fortune. I just *know things,* mom explains it to me like that.

Soran paid no attention to me and continued eating his peanut butter and jelly sandwich, but this was not the most intriguing characteristic of my new acquaintance. You see, I realized that I felt a weird sense of calm in the presence of Soran. Decorated by a tall chief-like feather that stuck out of his head, to the vividly rainbow-colored stripes of his body, he seemed familiar. *Have I met him before?* I cocked my head and turned to Wormly.

"I've never met actual creatures like you all before. Well, only in my imagination. Strange. I'm all set, but there is one thing. I will need some type of device to journal my adventures, like a recorder or pen and paper," I said as I prepared for the trip.

Scurrying and rustling immediately ensued at my request and an ant appeared with a large book and a rather strange writing utensil. The ant was like those I had spotted in the crowd earlier and about half my size. The book, well…the book was leather-bound and had the appearance of an old artifact from the rustic-look of the worn and tattered cover to the antique-colored pages. The journal had definitely been used. The pen was made of wood, carved in the shape of an ice-plant slide with ornately carved flowers resembling the plants and flowers of this new world I found myself in now. I picked up the book and pen. *Wow, they're heavy.* I felt like a king with such majestic-looking tools, but I couldn't possibly carry them throughout my journey, they were huge. I hand back the items to the ant.

"Are you kidding me? I cannot carry these, especially since I'm only 5 inches tall in your world. I shrank when I entered it, I guess? I need something smaller," I said.

"Yes, you are right, but you dare not wander around our world or outer worlds unprotected with Gonthragon out there. The journal has some protections, but we aren't sure what they are," Wormly said.

"Okay?" I said looking confused.

"We have planned for this trip for many years and I almost forgot, our royal coach shall carry you to the deepest reaches of our world," Wormly announced as three creatures pulled a leaf-shaped carriage right in front of me.

Wow. The carriage was beautiful. It appeared to be made of gold inlaid with intricately carved flowers and sticks, whilst the wheels were made of ice-plant vines, entwined with flowers.

"What are these little things?" I asked, petting them on the head.

"Oh, the antlings? They help transport items around our land and outer worlds," said Wormly.

My eyes filled with excitement and enlarged a bit as they do, when I can "see" things that others cannot. I felt my mysterious blue eye swirl around inside its socket as I looked at what appeared to be human-sized ants in comparison to me, Although I was the size of a bug, I was used to ants being small insects. I stepped up, sat down, and reached down to pet the antling.

"It's awesome! The antlings remind me of my pet dog, Sarah. She's about the same color too," I said.

"This is a special leaf carriage made especially for your journey. The flowers and Ice Plant vines are from our world. You might have noticed them earlier. While you're in the carriage, you're protected, but the journal offers its own protection too," Wormly said, handing me the journal and pen he had retrieved from the ant.

Protected? What do I need protection from?

Soran slid onto the lead ant. Smaller antlings lined up behind him. He took the reins and led us down the path that earlier carried the echo of Wormly's welcome. The sounds of goodbyes from the huge crowd soon become faint whispers in the air behind us.

CHAPTER

Divorce isn't the end of the world, sometimes it's the entrance to a new one.

—Darby Raju

"Ouch, oh…that really hurt. Sheesh, whoa, what happened?" I muttered as I questioned myself, whilst I struggled to get off the ground. *What just happened? I was heading down a path on a journey, my supposed destiny and well, was that real?*

I had never felt so foolish before and I hoped to not repeat it again. I'm not quite sure what hit me. It had been several minutes since I left home. *I knew I went somewhere. Was that one of my dreams? Was it real?*

I heard the tardy bell sound, the realization that I was late resounded with each echo. Once again, I would have sit a whole hour in detention with Terrance. We don't get along. Terrance, my school nemesis was more precise a description for him and everyone at school knew it.

I turned the corner of the school and could see my classroom door from inside the inner quad area, where I spend hours in "time-out." Mrs. G gripped the door and did not see me. She had just closed the door, which meant it was definitive, my fate of consequences in detention today and Terrance. Usually when I'm late and my teacher sees me, she'll slowly close the door, not today. Ugh! My hard work of trying to stay out of trouble had been thwarted by the closed door.

Even though it seemed to me that many of the kids in my school knew exactly which buttons to push to set me off, I had been doing better controlling my anger and staying out of trouble. I hated my life!

I entered the office to find Terrance already there. He took his detention slip, turned to me and taunted, "Loser, you always have to go to detention!"

Terrence? Ugh! Why did he have to see me arrive late? Out of all the kids at school, he was the only one that could irritate me to the point of trouble. My therapist said it was because we are so similar. We trigger each other. Our history of trips to the principal's office were legendary with the kids and staff. I had only been at this school a short period during the current school year. I transferred from another school because we moved.

Oh no, not now! I felt my face turn hotter, just like a volcano before it erupts. I knew I was angry. *Okay, okay, try to calm down, breathe,* I tell myself. Dang it. *Who was I kidding?* I was too stressed out and mad! My therapist told me to count to ten or take some deep breaths during times like these, but knowing and doing are two different things when it comes to being bipolar.

Although most psychiatrists don't diagnose children with bipolar disorder, my mom did extensive research at Stanford University. She said that the DSM-IV book listed bipolar disorder in children as a "not otherwise specified" disorder. Anyway, my dad was bipolar and my symptoms included my chaotic mind, *"irrational,"* and it cannot remember to be *"rational,"* as mom said. Bipolar for me meant mood swings, lots of them. My moods would swing from happy to sad quickly. Meltdowns were more of an accurate depiction, which consisted of me reacting to situations in an overdramatic way. Sometimes a bit sensitive and things get taken the wrong way. Therapy's helped me work on this as well as practicing coping skills.

Unpredictable was what my life was like living with bipolar disorder and I walked to the counter for my detention slip. Today, my day won't end at 2:30. I had to stay an hour after school.

As I entered my first class of the day, I slammed down my backpack on the desk due to my altercation with Terrance. I was furious with him and slumped in my seat. Mrs. G wasn't ready for this behavior today and the slightest thing would be my trigger.

Her hair was in a beehive style hairdo and she was dressed in her usual business attire with wire-rim glasses perched on the edge of her nose. She glared at me. The familiar motherly stare just before life turns chaotic and I knew it all too well. Mrs. G had given me this look before too and I knew what it meant. I had pushed the limits with her due to everything that took place today, all the stress in my life, and to top it all off, Terrance.

I screamed at her, "Don't glare at me!"

Mrs. G. pointed to the door and I knew that I needed space outside of class. I walked to the door leading outside, opened it, and turned to Mrs. G and shouted, "I don't care, I hate my life!" and slammed the door behind me.

Sitting outside gave me time away from everyone. Although I was irritated, my mind wandered, and I thought about this morning. So much had happened. It wasn't until now that I noticed a terrible pain on my left toe and I lightly massaged it. *Why was my foot hurting so badly? What happened? Wait a minute...thoughts of the day are really foggy. Had I traveled to another world in reality?* I couldn't remember exactly, but all I recalled was I walked to school and then it happened, that crazy Yesinia, the newest member of Mrs. G's class, hit me with her little sister's stroller. *But* I recalled a strange dark and cold place, hhhmmm, but I also had memories that I was relaxed and not anxious. *Where had I gone to feel that way? Was it a dream, my imaginary world or real? Hhhmmm.*

As I continued to relive the morning's events I felt my body calm down a bit. I was ready to join the class, but not quite sure where Mrs. G was in the curriculum as I re-entered the classroom.

"I want you to get into your buddy groups," Mrs. G announced.

I immediately felt my stomach as it cringed. My feelings were that I don't have a buddy in the world, let alone in this class. Nobody understood me. Currently, my emotions were all over the place, similar to curves on a roller coaster, every twist and turn of my life was unexpected and so were my emotions. I hated being bipolar and life was too difficult to deal with everyday situations that were a bit easier for most.

I reluctantly moved my chair to my group. As I did this, Terrence walked by and taunted me for a second time. He opened his eyes widely and stuck out his tongue, but this time I didn't react outwardly. I told myself, *Ignore him, read* over and over, whilst my insides were doing summersaults with my breakfast.

Yesinia, my partner, moved her chair closer to me and we took turns reading. The story was about Galileo and his telescope invention. It was her turn to read.

"According to Albert van Helden in 1977, it was Galileo who made the instrument famous. He constructed his first three-powered spyglass in June or July 1609, presented an eight-powered instrument to the Venetian Senate in August, and turned a twenty-powered instrument to the heavens in October or November...," Yesinia read on, but I was not listening. As always in my life, I tried to manage my anger inwardly. In a way it soothed me. As I imagined Galileo with his telescope, I tried to imagine his world whilst she read. I pretended I was Galileo and stood up and looked through a telescope. It appeared to be a type of time travel, if you will, but Yesinia was in my face now and disrupted my short-lived imaginary journey.

"What is wrong with you? It's your turn to read. Are you paying one bit of attention to me or are you just not able to read? Are you dumb?" she cascaded insult after insult.

She was annoyed by my daydreaming. I hated her. She was the oldest of six children and irritatingly bossy. Since my mother volunteered at the school, she knew information about some of the parents and their families. As for her, she had started only two weeks ago and already I had figured out she was no fun to work with at all!

I also had just started Lorn Edes School full-time, so she and I were partnered together. I had previously attended a Special Day School, but recently mainstreamed.

Yesenia had long black hair, which she tied up in pigtails and always wore the prettiest dresses. Today her dress was pink. Her face was as smooth as a baby's cheek. Her complexion a creamy white with small brown freckles. I secretly liked her, but would never let her know that. She annoyed me and I did not want to give her the satisfaction of being able to publicly humiliate me for my affections of her.

"I'm not dumb. Stop calling me dumb. Your dresses are dumb!" I responded to her torturous whining.

"Then read. It's your turn!" Yesinia said with an annoyed look on her face as she rolled her eyes, crossed her arms, slumped back in her chair and to add insult to injury, blew upward to cause her bangs to flutter over her forehead.

Although we were both irritated, I was more than her. We took turns reading, both pretended to get along for the rest of the period. Cooperation took all the strength I could muster.

The bell had rung for recess, which was the most challenging time of the school day for me. Socially, I was awkward and I don't have any friends. I learned in therapy that I need to work on communicating better and that interaction required the ability to read social cues. I really didn't know what that meant, but learned it meant knowing the flow of conversation. I struggled with this in school and it had been one reason why I didn't have many friends.

I loved playing tetherball though and I raced to be first in line, but I was too late! Terrence and Jorge had beaten me to the court. I had to wait patiently until my turn, which was not something that came naturally to me; it required loads of effort. Today, it was going to be a struggle.

"Ha, ha, you're out, who's my next victim?" bragged Terrence, as he beat Jorge in the third round.

Terrence was not only my nemesis, but the school bully. I talked about him extensively in therapy and I learned coping skills. I knew I should walk away and try to play another game and create distance between myself and Terrence; however, I wanted to beat him so badly!

"Hello Terrence, are you ready to meet your doom? I've been practicing and I'm going to whip your butt!" I taunted Terrence as he moved into the circle, because he triggered me twice today and I wanted revenge!

"Ha, it's you Joshua, you're going down!" Terrence responded.

We started to play our game, both eager to win and both equally skilled. It was neck and neck and neither one of us was going to give in. But just as I thought I had won, the ball hit my face. I felt my toe twinge for a second time today and then I fell to the ground. Terrence laughed, just as I hit the pavement. I saw his face. Now, there was a time when I would have risen up and attempted to annihilate him, but I have practiced the art of self-control. I got up and rushed over to the Peace Makers.

"Hey, I need help. Terrence hit me in the face with the tetherball and then started laughing. We are supposed to work on getting along and he's teasing me," I explained.

The school just started a new program designed by the school district to help students with conflict resolution and the Peace Makers were a pair of students, given the job to help their peers with conflict. They were recognized on the playground by their rainbow-colored striped shirts and feather-decorated pens. I just stared at them with a gaze of wonderment. Something about their appearance caused me to immediately begin to whirl around and my head began to spin. I felt as though I was inside Galileo's telescope I read about earlier and had been shot into the air like a rocket!

CHAPTER

I really didn't understand at first. But as the years went by, I thought it was my fault. It was a very confusing time for me.

—Anonymous eighteen-year old boy

hew...swish...swirly...poing...POP! I fell into the seat of a golden carved leaf and checked myself to make sure I was all in one piece. The image of the rainbows and feathered pens previously in my view, now transformed to the back of the head of someone seemingly familiar, but the surroundings were vastly different! Soran, the one I had met earlier today and the one I sought for protection just moments earlier, the spiritual healer and the Peace Maker. *I got it, they are dressed the same.* It was then that I pulled on the reins and the driver immediately stopped.

"Is there something I can do for you?" asked Soran.

He had jelly all over his face and giant flies were swarming around his head.

"No, no, just drive," I whispered and let out a sigh of disbelief and frustration.

I sat and pondered. I placed my hand on my head, my elbow on my knee, and raised my foot onto a foot-railing inside the carriage. I tried to piece it all together in a way that made sense to me. Of course, nothing about being the size of a human bug or riding through a telescope or taking a fall to gain access to different worlds was "nonsensical" by any stretch of the imagination.

When I returned to both my human world and my imaginary world, I'm in exactly the same spot and it seemed nobody noticed I was gone. But why am I slipping in and out of this world? What's causing this to happen? Is this a dream or real? It seemed that each time I get hurt or suffer emotionally, it was then that I traveled between these two worlds, depending on where I was. What did this mean? I jotted down notes of these thoughts and the day's venture thus far in my journal, in hopes they would help me figure it all out.

Soran continued to drive the carriage along the path. We had traveled a great deal of distance from the original spot of my journey into my new world, or so it felt that way to me. All the while I took notes.

The trail was laid crosswise with narrow vines, over which chicken wire was lain to improve traction. My thoughts were interrupted by my observation of my immediate surroundings. Thick green moss overgrew the ice plant spears and care was needed, especially this morning when dew created a surface that was treacherously slick.

Suddenly! The wheels of the carriage slipped and I felt myself fall, carriage and all…down…down…down. The rush sent my mind racing.

"Aaaahhhhh, Soran, do something—quickly! We are going to die!" I heard myself scream. Fear quickly overtook my body. *Oh no, I'm going to die. Nobody is even going to miss me, but mom is going to be so sad, especially since dad left. What is down there? Am I going to hit bottom? What if Gonthragon is down there, what will happen then? I cannot be defeated by a fall. I have to survive this. Help*! I screamed again for Soran to do something, but my thoughts of never returning home and dying in this world held me captive.

Yet the carriage and I continued to fall. The pace quickened every second for what seemed like an eternity.

Then, most eerily, the carriage stopped, in midair, flipped over, and crashed down!

"Great, face down in the thicket of shrubs. Now what?" I asked rhetorically.

As I peered outside of the carriage, I noticed a trail. The trail ascended and then descended gradually, parallel to a creek, and then opened into a clearing, near where there appeared to be a small cabin. I got out and walked carefully. I paused every few feet to scan the forest on both sides for any sign of life. I knew well that the odds of seeing something of interest were directly proportional to time spent looking. *Thanks, Mrs. G.*

The wind began to howl, which slightly frightened me and I fell off my feet and injured my hand as I toppled down the side of a rock. There were several sharp objects, including sharp tree branches. A gashed wound was the result. Only bleeding mildly, I felt fine and brushed off the blood onto my pants. I quickly jumped back to my feet and observed my surroundings for any sign of an intruder. The hairs on my arm stood on end. I knew something was out there watching and waiting. Maybe I couldn't see it, but my eye sensed a shadow, something dark even from this far away. Mom told me that my eye may one day begin to act strangely, especially when it came to dark forces. Spinning around was only the beginning to the strange things my eye had done, but I needed to ask her more about that. The feeling, as I peered, was eerie, like someone was breathing in my ear and had eyes in my face. I felt danger. We had to leave immediately.

"Soran, Soran! I need something to protect us," I whispered loudly. "There's something out there I just know it. Get my journal and some sort of weapon. Writing down what's happening can bring spiritual support or at least I was told by an older person sometime in my life. We can't be sure what we may be up against," I told him, convinced of my feelings. Soran moved quickly, turned the carriage right side up with the help of the ant-lings and then rummaged through our belongings until he found the ice plants and spirit sticks. He picked up the journal, my pen and spears, and gave them to me.

Suddenly, the bushes beside the cabin rustled. I saw something weird hiding. Soran whistled and out came a one-eyed periwinkle-colored creature with a long blue polka-dotted elephant nose poking through the bush. Its orange eye had the most beautiful lashes and the rest of its body was shaped like a duck-bill platypus. It had a long, green swishy tail and eight legs. Soran said it was a Gombi.

I looked at him and asked, "What in the world is a Gombi?"

"That creature is a Gombi," he said pointing straight at the creature. "They are shy and sensitive. Norkels keep them as pets and supply them with food," Soran explained.

"Uh Soran, Wormly mentioned I was in the land of the Norkels, but I saw several creatures back where we met. What specifically are Norkels?" I asked, just as confused at the mention of Gombis, but at this moment, all the inhabitants of this world had been different than my typical dog or cat.

"Norkels are kindly strange folk, they live in Green Burrough Valley, which is part of the Ice Plants' land. They are short people with large fat noses, two large green eyes, no hair, and three-toed large hairy feet and long arms with four fingers.

"Hahaha, I would love to see those, Wait …weren't there a few Norkels back where we first met?" I asked.

"Yes, a few," Soran said and then went on. "They wear soft tree bark type robes with dark green ties made of shed Gombi tails. They eat insects and worms and save Googoo bird eggs for the Gombi to eat," Soran explained as we walked up to a cabin.

"W-w-what? Googoo bird eggs? I'm still processing Norkels and now what did you say? Gombi? Soran—" I was cut off, he turned around and placed his finger across his lips.

"Ssshhh," Soran said as the Gombi approached me. The Gombi seemed to be as frightened of me as I was of it at first. Soran began communicating with the Gombi as he gently brushed against its tail and it seemed less intimidated.

"He knows we are friendly now," whispered Soran.

Soran convinced the Gombi we meant no harm. *I'm still curious about Norkels. I need to know more.*

"Norkels are in the land of the Ice Plants, Green Burrough Valley and…," I started to ask Soran, but all I got was a stare and silence.

He took a hold of my hand and tugged on my arm, and guided me to the nearest cabin. I felt as though we were being watched and that several little eyes were upon our backs. Soran said we would be safe in the cabin.

Entering the cabin we were met by an old woman with scraggly purple hair partially pinned up in a bun, the remaining greasy strands danced in the air like snakes on her head. She wore a tattered oversized flowing purple gown that matched her hair and brown wrinkled skin.

"My dearest boy, please come forth," she gestured with a soft voice. "I am Pergita, but most call me the wise old one."

Usually, as I had said before, strange folk, places, and events would have caused me to enter into a highly anxious state, but I was used to it by now.

"Hello Pergita. I'm Joshua, I'm trying to find my way back, but I've come to explore your world a bit with Soran...," I began.

"Joshua, I have been in contact with Wormly through the medium of tea leaves and they revealed to him that your presence here is both a blessing and a curse," Pergita explained.

"Tea leaves, how do you communicate through leaves? A blessing would be nice, but I've had enough of curses, so don't tell me that!" I said.

"The blessing is you. You see the Norkels have been under attack by the Thragons and they have caused a great disturbance in our world, causing the mood to become subdued and unfriendly," she explained.

"What kind of disturbance?" I asked. *Moods? I struggle with being moody too, my psychologist is working with me on that.*

"Fire, destruction, mind-control. We are protected within the confines of our cabins, but once in the outlands or other regions, we begin to lose ourselves and we risk becoming transformed into one of them—a Thragon," Pergita said as she motioned with her arms in a gesture meaning the whole land.

"Transformed, you mean like I have become a bug-sized boy?" I asked, staring down at my body, realizing again how small I was.

"When they see into our world, it's like they see into our minds. They take it over, and we transform. Their ruler, Gonthragon, can see into our world, although we aren't quite sure how." Pergita was walking around placing her hands on her head, and as she said the word "transform," her body magically changed.

"What the heck?" I said witnessing Pergita's body shape into a creature with bat-like wings, sharp teeth and claws, and horns atop her head. She gritted her teeth. I jumped back and fell over Soran. We both toppled to the ground.

As I stood up, Pergita continued, "We need your help to travel to the Grasslands, find out what he's up to and stop him. You are the key to the survival of our way of life and the very lives of our people."

I didn't know what to say and stood still for several minutes. I walked to the door and opened it. I was gently reminded of the ruins of our carriage as I saw it laying there and then that familiar sensation of "being watched" overcame me again. I felt myself fall to the ground, once again…as I was transported back to my world.

CHAPTER 5

There is no such thing as a "broken family." Family is family and is not determined by marriage certificates, divorce papers, and adoption documents. Families are made in the heart. The only time family becomes null is when those ties in the heart are cut. If you cut those ties, those people are not your family. If you make those ties, those people are your family. And if you hate those ties, those people will still be your family because whatever you hate will always be with you.

—Unknown Internet source

I felt my body warm and lying horizontally in what appeared to be grass. As I opened my eyes, I noticed I was lying in a large field, blades of dry grass surrounded me. Not a soul was in sight and it was obvious that I was not at home or school, I was still in this world, but where? *Where on earth am I? Come to think of it, am I still on planet earth? I feared for my life. Previously, I had been transported to my world, but it's clear, I'm somewhere entirely different.*

"Soran!" I call as loudly as I can. "Is anyone there?" I asked in panic mode.

The same weird sensation I felt just moments earlier enveloped my whole body. I passed out once more.

Again, I woke up in unfamiliar surroundings. This time, I faced and looked straight up. I noticed the ceiling was alive as the worms crawled over each other, intertwining themselves, as they crawled along the walls and into the corners. I heard a loud squawk that caused me to jump out of my skin. My body began to shake and shiver. I saw shadows cast along the walls where the worms crawled. They moved in the shape of something large and frightening. I picked myself up and rushed into the opposite corner and cowered. Darkness in the form of a shadow emerged. A gigantic hand took a handful of worms from the moving wall and threw them out of the dungeon-like windows, where bars had been bent, as if something had escaped from inside.

"Oh God," I said quietly so nobody could hear me.

Whatever was making the noise outside of the wall stopped. As I listened, I heard slurping noises…it must have devoured the worms, moments later, it continued squawking again.

The room was sweltering and I began to sweat. The sensation I had felt twice earlier today had begun to take over my body. I felt as if my entire soul was depressed and death would soon be upon me. I recalled what Wormly had said about the Thragons and their king. *Lord, help me. Tell me I'm not going to run into him,* I told myself, trying to calm myself down. The room had begun to boil with heat. My clothes were drenched from both the heat and from fear of seeing this monster! My knees gave way and buckled. I fell to the floor. A monster entered.

It stood towering over me and as I glanced up, I noticed it wore a dark robe and its eyes glowed with flames, causing me to flinch. I couldn't meet its gaze. I wished it would vanish, but closed eyes heightened all other senses, especially sound. Its bat-like wings scratched the ground as it dragged them across the floor, circling me where I lay. Fearful, I wondered what kind of a creature this was. As it passed me, it sniffed my body, lifting me three feet off the ground as its nose stuck to my clothes. Shocked, my eyes blinked open briefly. Its breath smelled like old rotten eggs. Its black scaly skin smelled like month-old maggoty dead meat. I gagged. And if I weren't scared enough to death by its appearance, it spoke with a raspy, scratchy deep voice, which caused me to shake.

"My name is Gonthragon and I am the ruler of the Thragons and this land," he spat into my ear.

I thought I was going to pee my pants!

"Do you know why I brought you here boy?" he questioned me.

I could not speak nor glance at it.

"It is you I seek to take over these worlds, since you are the only one who holds the power to help me unlock the secret of the universe! You must come with me to my chamber. I have something to *show you*," he screeched into my ear as he spat burning hot rancid liquid into my face.

I reached up and quickly used my shirt to wipe my face. The burning didn't subside. I noticed a piece of my skin bloodied on my shirt. My face had really begun to burn. I thought, *I have to get out of here!*

The gargoyle, which had reentered the room after its meal, dragged me by my arm forcing me to follow Gonthragon.

Wait, what? I know that's bad news. I don't remember where, but I know I've heard those words. They seemed familiar... When someone says they have something to show you, they usually mean harm... Was this a faded memory from my childhood or was this something I'd learned recently? I really couldn't remember, but I wasn't about to let this ogre take over the world of the Norkels or mine. This meant war and I wasn't going quietly. I felt into my pocket. There was an ice plant spear that Soran must have put in my pocket. Now I could fight back with my secret weapon.

My spear was special according to Wormly. It shrinks, transforms, and grows with the needs presented to it. Currently, I needed it to be small and fit into my pocket, so magically it did. *If I needed it to grow larger it would. My need is what guides this spear.*

"Uh, I think you have me confused with someone else," I responded to him.

I'm scared, but I'm ready.

We walked into another room with what appeared to be dark, red blood that flowed from the walls. I glanced down as I felt something stinging my legs.

"Aaahhh!" I screamed, as I kicked off the large scorpions that crawled up my legs with every step I took.

Maybe I should close my eyes, but that only increased my hearing sense. As I stepped, the sound was grotesque as I stepped on something crunchy. I opened my eyes to larger than normal cockroaches that crunched below my feet, since there were so many covering the ground and they oozed black blood! I looked up, trying to avoid the site my prints are leaving behind and I noticed a large throne made of smooth black stones, which sat in the corner of the room. Bloodied Gombi fur draped over the back of the throne, the site made my stomach churn, but that was not all there appeared to be. Norkel skulls were nailed all around it too. The eerie feeling just kept getting worse. I wanted to escape!

I hastened my pace and stepped even further forward. I noticed a swirling white mist that surrounded the throne. The closer I got to it, the cooler I felt, all the while shivering not only from the cold, but the fear that continued to swell inside me. I found the temperature change a bit odd as the rest of the room was still sweltering and hot like lava.

As I examined the room, my body temperature fluctuated. I forgot I was not alone. Suddenly, the gargoyle pushed me toward the throne, which was where Gonthragon sat holding a large rod. The rod was covered in black spikes and had a small glass-like orb embedded in a silver casing on the top of it. For a moment, it flashed red, just like the eye of Gonthragon, but when I looked away and then back again, it appeared to be just a clear glass orb.

"Do you see this boy? I want you to gaze into it and tell me what you see," he insisted and placed the orb in a holder near his throne.

I stood in place. The gargoyle came up behind me and pushed me yet again. I had no choice. I walked closer to the orb and my eye began to swirl in its socket once again. Gonthragon didn't notice this as my back was to him. My eye reflected the eye in the orb and showed me this:

Me walking up to it, placing my eye upon the orb and being sucked into the orb. The orb began to spin and my spirit from within me began to flow toward it, becoming one with it, and then the worse thing transpired next! Gonthragon became a monstrous fire-breathing dragon and set fire to the ice plants. Next, he flew to, what appeared to me, the center of the Earth and caused the core to become so hot it exploded upon itself and then the vision was gone. Then, suddenly another image appears (I felt more relaxed with this vision). My spear was in my hand and I stabbed Gonthragon in the chest and turned to face the orb.

Quickly, I stabbed the center of the orb, Gonthragon disappeared and I returned to my home. Whilst I observed the vision, he must have sensed my next steps as he immediately rushed over toward me to guard his throne.

I remembered that I had the spear in my pocket and thoughts of what had been transporting me to and from the two worlds entered my mind. I thought I would give it a try and I stabbed my foot with the spear.

"AAAHHHHHH!"

CHAPTER

I cry at night when I'm in bed, but my mom never knows.

—Anonymous four-year-old girl

The bell rang, just as Terrence was called over by the Peace Makers to discuss his inappropriate remarks to me. "Terrence, you know we have talked to you about using inappropriate comments and being competitive with Joshua. You have now violated our request for the second time. We've talked to the principal and she said you'll have detention today," said the Peace Maker.

I'd usually be happy about this, but my mind was not in this world, not now. How could it be? I had more important things to worry about now.

My plan worked, yes! I thought I would be trapped in Gonthragon's throne! Whew, I'm glad to be out of there, but what about the Norkels and Wormly? I can't let them suffer and what about that vision? Man ...that was something else. I cannot imagine what would happen if Gonthragon could take over this world, let alone mine. Civilization as we know it would be destroyed and how could I live with myself then? I seriously hoped he's trapped there and couldn't transcend his world into mine. My thoughts were interrupted...

"Joshua, you can go back to class now and don't play tetherball with Terrence. If we see you two on the same court, you both will be banned for two months," the Peace Maker warned me.

"Yeah, okay," I said turning to walk to class.

My stomach twisted at the thought of seeing Terrence again in detention. *I hoped they separate us; I really don't feel like I can ignore him today.*

The day finally came to an end and I placed the remaining homework paper into my backpack and headed for detention. I entered, signed in, and stared at the clock. Really, I didn't even notice when 3:30 came. I daydreamed the whole time and relived the scene in Gonthragon's throne room. The bell sounded and I was so happy to have my torture end. On my way, I stopped and stared at the stony pavement where my journey had begun. *Had it really only been this morning?* I could be sent back since I knew causing myself great pain or emotional sadness would help me go back and forth between worlds. Well, it worked once at my will, but I wanted to be sure I was ready.

When I looked into Gonthragon's eye today, I noticed something with my own eyes. I'm sure it was because they were special. I have two differently colored eyes. Many people have questioned me, but mom said that it had always been that way and they are magical in some way. I knew there was more to the story. Mom was the source of knowledge. I wanted to find out more. I know that there was something mysterious about them and my adventures today made me all the more curious about it.

I went to unlock the door, but found I didn't need to use my key because the door was unlocked and brushed open with the slightest touch. Inside I saw my mother and father. My dad was clutching onto his packed bags. My mom was crying. All thoughts of Gonthragon and school evaded my mind and my parents took hold of me.

"Mom, dad…what's going on?" I began to cry.

Nobody answered me. Maybe they hadn't heard me. *Didn't they know I was missing? Hhmm, well, my traveling from world to world happened inside of one school day, so perhaps not.*

I felt emptiness inside my body and my spirit was instantly blackened. I saw that my dad was moving out today and the divorce became more real to me.

"Please don't go dad. I know you two can make things work. Mom, tell him," I pleaded.

"Joshua, we both love you. Don't worry, it's going to be tough at first, but you will see your dad and me both. Your father will set up his place and then you'll see him. Right Jake?" Mom advised.

"Yes, son. You know you and your sister will spend time with your old dad. Talk to Jonah and Jada if they aren't too busy, they can come too. But in the meantime, listen to your mom and do your homework. I love you!" my father replied.

My dad got up and I walked into the den to look out the window. Meanwhile Jada and Jonah walked in from school.

"Josh, what's up?" Jonah asked, lightly punching me on the arm as Jada walked into the other room with Leilani.

"Dad's really leaving, did you know?" I asked him.

"Well, you knew they were getting a divorce. We found out earlier. It sucks, but we'll be fine. You doin' okay?" Jonah asked looking more sympathetic.

"No," I said and headed down the hall, but stopped as I heard Leilani and Jada talking in their room. Poking my nose into my sister's room, I asked, "Did you know dad's leaving?"

"Do you know how to knock?" Jada asked, slamming the door in my face.

"Don't do that Jada. He's depressed and needs to talk to us," Leilani told Jada and opened the door again.

"We were just talking about dad leaving," Leilani said.

"Yeah, Jonah and I were talking about it, but I'm still sad," I said, sitting next to Leilani on Jada's bed.

"Josh, grow up. It's going to be okay. Stop whining!" Jada raised her voice to me and rolled her eyes.

"Jada, you are so mean. You know he's super sensitive! Dang, be nice. It does suck," Leilani said, patting me on the back.

Jada got up from the bed and walked in front of Leilani and me.

"Mom and my dad split up. Do you see me crying? Yes, I miss him, but I moved on with my life. Your dad was okay to us, but you'll move on too," Jada said as she continued to place pictures in a photo frame for her wall.

"Jada didn't mean it. We will all see dad and it's going to work out," Leilani said.

"How do you figure, it bites," I replied, slamming the door, hanging my head and walking back into the front room. Leilani's eyes followed me as I exited the room.

I stood there, heartbroken as my dad gathered the last of his belongings and loaded them into his car.

"Can I help you take your stuff to your car, dad?" I asked.

"Sure Josh my man. Take that one suitcase over there for your old dad?" he said.

Carrying my dad's suitcase gave me an opportunity to place something inside it and it took only a second.

"Dad?" I said.

"Yes, what's up son?" dad responded looking at me.

"When am I going to see you?" I inquired.

"Well, it's going to take me a few weeks to get settled now that I think of it. Your mom and I will talk about it and let you know. Now I have to go. You should do your homework," my dad said, as he placed items into the car, seeming to not care to hug me.

Sad, I turned to the house. As I walked back in, I noticed everyone in the house seemed so sad. My sister Leilani moved to the couch and flipped pages on family albums. It seemed to recall our family adventures.

Jonah began playing a song on the piano, which made mom cry. It was, "Proud of your boy," a song he sang for her in the choir.

Jada sat next to Leilani and fixed pictures that had strayed from their position in the albums.

"Josh, do you remember going to the theme park with dad? You two posed with Star Wars characters? Here are the photos. They'll make you smile," Leiliani said, trying to be kind.

"That was a happy time, I remember," I said as I stood watching everyone.

Leilani's face showed intermittent signs of happiness, followed by sadness, as I watched her perusing the albums. Mom headed to the kitchen and started washing dishes or cooking as I'm not sure which event was caused by the banging in the kitchen.

I staggered to my room, climbed onto my bed to peer outside of my window. I caught the last bit of my father as he closed the trunk. He turned his head, walked to the driver's side door. My overwhelmed anxious feeling started and I knocked on my window to get his attention. He must have heard me as he jerked his head around, his eyes finally landing on me. He stopped, pointed to me, and then hugged himself; a gesture to hug me.

Standing in front of the window, I stared as the car disappeared down the street. Desires to bolt outside and run down the street were overtaken by my drained body, apparently very tired, I drifted off into a bit of a daydream, but was interrupted.

"Josh, come on!" mom screamed.

"What? I'm coming!" I hollered back.

"Okay, just come on, it's your favorite!" mom said turning back around to go back to the kitchen.

Focusing after an emotional episode was always difficult for me, but I walked down the hall and into the kitchen. Sitting at the table I noticed she made spaghetti and salad. I loved her cooking! Well, except for the salad. I don't particularly like vegetables, but I know they are good for me and she only made me eat them because she loved me. "Mom, can you tell me again about my eye?" I asked, trying to finish my salad first.

She looked like she had been crying for a while, which I hadn't noticed before and sounded like her nose was stuffed up. She always sounded that way when she was sad, which usually accompanied crying a lot. "There you are, sleepy head, were you off on another adventure in your dreams? I know you love your imaginary play, even in your dreams," she told me.

"Mom, please tell me more about my eye." I begged her.

"What do you want to know Josh?" she quietly responded. "What happened to my eye and why are they different colors?" I asked. Tears welled up in my mother's eyes and her expression grew solemn.

"Parks were a place you really enjoyed," she began "especially running around on the play structures. Remember?"

"I remember the Pepsi Park. You and dad used to take us there. I remember you chasing us," I said with a smile.

"Yes, you loved me to chase you and try and catch you. Do you remember the monster game and troll under the bridge?"

"Yes, that was my favorite thing to do there."

My mom used to run around and chase us, trying to catch us on the play structures. The Pepsi Park had a bridge that was about 4 feet long and curved upward. She used to go underneath and pretend to be a troll. I remembered how scared I was of going across and her catching me, catching us. *Those were fun times!*

"We used to go and play baseball games too. You guys used to love the park," Mom reminded me.

"Oh yeah, I could never hit the ball, so I used to run to the tire swing, leaving everyone on the baseball field. Then everyone would run over. You would push all four of us on the tire swing. We would get so dizzy and then try to play troll under the bridge, you would catch our feet," I said.

"Well, it was during one of those times, you fell off of the play structure at the park and I took you to the hospital. They determined you needed eye surgery. You were only two," she said, hugged me, and then cleaned up the dishes on the counter. "You were very lucky and almost lost your eye and the ability to see."

"I don't remember that. Mom, I have both of my eyes now, so what else happened?" I asked impatiently.

"Doctors were surprised that at the same time you arrived, there was an older man, like a Shaman.

"What's a Shaman?" I asked.

"A Shaman can see things hidden from others and predict the future or speak for the gods," mom explained.

Wow, predict the future. Is that what I saw in my vision? Was that a prediction?

"Your eye needed replacing and by sheer luck the old Shaman, that was in the hospital at the same time, died. He had perfect eyes and vision. However, his eyes were blue, and yours were brown," she said as she gazed into my eyes in a way to make me feel scared and jittery.

My mom's eyes can grow very large, and she was a bit scary that way. For the longest time I remembered, when she would put me to bed, she would get super close to my eyes, say, "Good night, sleep tight, don't let the bedbugs bite!" She scared me, so I would pull the covers up to my ears for fear of a monster climbing into bed with me or worse, a bedbug!

My mom stopped and looked directly at me and into my eyes, "So it has been rumored that this Shaman could see the truth in everything and brought justice to many lives. The doctor's joked about it and said that you would carry on this tradition in your life," mom explained.

"Really?" I said, turning my head to the side a bit.

"Yes, but I'm not sure I believe that, but a warning was also given that you shouldn't be misled if someone wanted to *"show you something."* This would mean they intend on doing harm to someone or to you. Do you remember now?" she questioned, looking at me.

"Hhmm, no, I don't remember, but thanks mom. It all makes sense to me. I love you!" I said.

"What makes sense to you Josh? Uh, I love you too," she hollered back as she walked into the kitchen again.

I really wanted to find a way to have my dad back and my family whole again, but this wouldn't matter if the world as I knew it ended. So I made a decision to get back and help the Norkels. I already knew that I needed great distress to get back! I just had to make something big happen!

Night wasn't coming fast enough! I wanted to fall asleep quickly and for tomorrow to start. I needed to get started on my plan!

CHAPTER

I was real young. I didn't know what was
going on. I knew Dad was missing, but I
didn't know why.

—Anonymous eight-year-old girl

I did not remember my dream from last night, but this
morning I rushed to school dazed and not really paying
attention to anything or anyone. I'm surprised I did not
trip again near the Ice Plants. I stopped and stared as I passed
by the land in which I fell into just the day before, the land of
the Ice Plants.

W-w-wait a minute. Those are Ice Plants! This is my world, so how are those here? Wow, we have Ice Plants too! Exciting and weird! I must make it on time and not be late.

I succeeded in my mission and as I entered class, Mrs. G told us about the lesson for the day.

"We are going to use the Smartboard to learn fractions," Mrs. G began. As I pulled out my notebook and a pencil, she continued.

"Remember to underline the new words we are learning today, put them in your vocabulary notebook. So the number on the top of the fraction is called the *numerator*, jot that down in your notes," she said, pointing to the Smartboard and her example. She then showed us the denominator, we wrote that down too.

"First you want to find a common denominator in both your numerator and denominator," explained Mrs. G, as she clicked the denominator and numerator with her expo marker, highlighting them.

I stopped listening and taking notes. I had a plan to carry out.

My eyes wandered around the room and I stopped to focus on Terrence. I knew that the only way my father would return home was if there was a major incident at school. He always came in emergency situations, family meant everything to him. A lightbulb flashed above my head as the idea hit me. *I needed to trigger Terrence, but how? I paused, thinking it over. Oh, yes, he hated it when I stared at him and made faces.* Putting my genius plan into action, I caught his attention as I flipped up my eyelids, squished my face and stuck out my tongue. Terrance saw me as he turned his head toward me. His face twisted and he began to turn red. He sprung out of his seat and almost flew as he launched himself toward my desk. *I imagined him toppling over everyone while students in the rows between us placed their feet in the isle.* But I awoke from my daydream to find him near me. My leg was actually still in the isle, and then it happened—*kablam!* He fell to the ground, hitting a desk on his way down!

"Aaaahhhhhhh!" screamed Yesenia who was closest to Terrence. It was her desk he hit, but not only that. Yesenia's desk always had knick-knacks on it. Today she had a metal Hello Kitty pencil case with slots for scissors, sharpened pencils, and other supplies. It looked like she was fully supplied today.

"Oh my gosh, what in the world? Call the office immediately, Jacob!" screamed Mrs. G.

I couldn't believe it! Oh no, blood streamed through the air, landed on my arm, and I squirmed inside. The site of blood, especially in large quantities, made me nauseous.

I watched the deep, red gushing liquid pour all over the floor and onto Yesenia's and my desk. Terrence lay in a puddle of blood. His eye was red. This plan all happened so fast and none of it matched what was imagined in my mind.

The whole class reacted as if they had just witnessed a murder, screaming, running, crying, yelling at me, and trying to get close enough to Terrance.

"Josh, what did you do?" asked a male voice.

"What's wrong with you? You're an idiot?" said another of my classmates.

"Oh my God, did he die?" questioned a screaming girl.

Mrs. G rushed to the phone, called the office, and moments later I heard sirens in the air. The scene was surreal, foggy. The student's voices were muffled by the sound of me talking to myself.

I hated myself so much for causing this problem. It's not bad enough that everyone didn't like me, now they hated me.

EMTs from Regional Ambulance entered the classroom quickly, checked Terrance's vitals, put him on the stretcher, and exited the room. Mr. Kewl, a tall built black male security guard wearing a bright-orange vest, entered as they left, followed by Mr. Ernie, a short soccer coach, well-known for the strength of ten horses. Everyone that was huddled to one side of the room pointed toward me. I was taken, dragged was more like it, to the office.

Raising my head, while being dragged to the office, I noticed the EMT putting Terrance inside the ambulance. I knew what laid ahead for me was going to be something awful. *How could I have done this? This wasn't like me. I never wanted him to get hurt!* I felt really bad as I entered the office. My imagination continued to wonder about my punishment. I waited for my parents to arrive.

Great, now mom and dad were going to be seriously disappointed in me. I couldn't do anything right. I thought of all the blood. I mean, I didn't hit him, he just fell. How could I ever live with myself after I triggered him and caused this to happen?

I continued to ponder my own destiny and what awaited me, but my thoughts were interrupted by voices, I believed from my mother and father arguing. The voices continued to get closer and closer.

"Well, he wouldn't have gone to school upset if you didn't just leave," my mom yelled at my dad.

My parents stormed into the room and sat opposite of me, staring at me as the sound of sirens faded down the street. My intention was for my father to return, but not like this. In my mind, I knew my parents could make things work out. They don't know they still love each other, but I did. By the looks on their faces, I had failed once again.

If I didn't already know I was in serious trouble, I could tell when Mrs. W entered the main office and called my parents inside of hers. The illusion that my parents would be ecstatic when they saw each other supporting and loving me was only in my mind. The idea that this "event" could bring them back together, quickly became a dream as my parents exited Mrs. W's office about twenty minutes after they entered.

My mom looked irritated and defeated at the same time. Her eyes were squinted, lips puckered, like she just ate a lemon, and her face was red with sweat across her forehead. My dad was supporting my mom's arm and he too looked a bit enraged, a look I knew all too well. We looked the same when we were mad, scowled faces, raised eyebrows, and definitely sweat over our entire face. Instead of walking, he seemed to march or pace alongside my mother.

"Joshua, get up, move it!" my mother said to me as she exited the office.

I cautiously got up and walked out, kept pace with my parents, but remained behind them. Nobody spoke as we left the school grounds and walked down the street toward home.

When we got home, mom walked into the kitchen, got some water, and sat down at the kitchen table. Dad and I entered the kitchen and sat down too.

My mom began, as she always did, "Josh, we aren't sure what happened today, but this is serious. Your father and I have to deal with your situation. You will no longer be attending Lorn Edes School."

"I want to say I'm sorry to Terrance, I feel bad," I said.

"You should feel bad. It's serious. Now, go to your room, I'll put on dinner. Your dad and I have things to discuss," Mom said.

"Can I tell you what happened?" I asked quietly, since I knew I was in serious trouble.

"What can you say? You've gotten angry at kids before, this isn't new. But this time, you've made a poor choice and it's serious! Terrance could have long-term damage," my mom said.

Walking down the corridor of the hall seemed to take forever. I paused to look at family portraits and pictures along the way. Thoughts of the other world filtered into my thoughts of my family.

My plan wasn't working in the slightest and all I wanted was to return to the world of the Norkels, to save everyone and in turn, save my family. Feelings of helplessness overtook my thoughts.

The pity started. *I really don't have any friends, my parents don't love me, and I would be better off left in the world of the Ice Plants! Well, I know my parents love me, but it's a struggle I'm faced with daily. It must be one of the reasons I take meds every day. Mom said dad felt the same way I do, like we don't have friends and like nobody understands or loves us. I hate being bipolar.*

I fell asleep on my bed.

"Josh, come on, dinnertime," Leilani whispered.

Sleeping deeply didn't come naturally to me and tonight not at all, since it was easy for Leilani to wake me up. She was being nice to me, something she did when I was upset or traumatic life events happened, which were more and more frequent since we found out that I suffered from a "not otherwise specified" disorder. We just called it bipolar. My dad was diagnosed with this too.

Leilani and I walked down the hall and into the den. Jada and Jonah met us there. We all sat down to pizza and my punishment immediately ensued. My mother and father revealed more bad news.

"Joshua, the principal has recommended expulsion from the school for your ill behavior. Your father and I have discussed alternatives. There's another school, which is further away that helps students with emotional disturbances. You're going to Seneca Academy," my mother explained.

"Josh, this school will help you son," my dad said empathetically.

"Where is the school mom? Can he still walk to it?" Leilani asked.

My mind wandered and I partially listened while I thought of my destiny, which I didn't believe would take place in this new school.

"No, it's in Fremont, two cities over, and he'll have to take a bus there," mom explained.

Wait, bus, did they say bus?

"A bus, what? Why can't you take me mom?" I questioned with a whine.

"Josh?" my mother said with that tone. I knew I should just close my mouth.

Although I had committed a terrible act against Terrance and gotten kicked out of the school, my family still loved me. I slouched in my chair and as always, began to daydream, but then got up and walked out of the den.

The edge of life and the edge of my daydreams seemed to collide. Everything in my world was in turmoil. Blackened spirits entered my mind, suffocating my thoughts, feelings. The floor hit my backside hard as I landed with a thud!

I must have looked extremely distraught and the situation must have been serious, since all my siblings walked into the room.

"Josh! Mom screamed as she rushed over and helped me.

"Oh God, get him up!" dad yelled.

"I'm okay, I'm okay, don't hover over me, give me some space!" I said irritated.

Leilani walked over, put her hand on my shoulder, hugged me and said, "Are you okay? You need to stop losing your focus, clear your mind! Remember, I'm here Josh, I'm here."

"Josh, what are you worrying about? Hey! You're going to do great things, you'll make new friends!" dad said.

I took deep breaths, paced the floor, focused on my family and responded, "I'm okay."

Jada and Jonah walked over and we all alternatively shared group hugs. I cherished these family moments, these are the times I loved. But the moment was to be ruined. My father had more bad news to tell us. He always had poor timing.

"I know this isn't the best news to deliver today, but I think you all should know," my dad shocked us.

Everyone stopped, turned to look at him, and he continued.

"Since we are all here I thought I'd tell you. I'm moving up north to Eureka," dad said and lowered his head. He always did this when he said something upsetting. "Dad, why are you moving away? You said it was going to take you a few weeks to set up. You never said you were moving out of the city. Where is Eureka and when are we going to see you? Don't you love us anymore?" inquired Leilani.

Such questions escaped my sister's mouth, but were in my mind too. Could life get any more complicated? I just wanted to die.

The mood became more subdued in the house. *Why on earth is my life sucking so dreadfully right now? I am trying to get my parents together, not push my dad further away.*

"Dad, no, you can't. Josh needs you, and so do I," begged Leilani.

Leilani was upset and as my mother reassured my sister, my father escaped the house, leaving us all to dwell in this land of misery. This was not my plan!

Jada, Jonah, mom, and I all hugged Leilani, she needed it.

I asked to sleep on the floor in my mom's room, which was where I felt the safest, while my sister also slept in my mom's room next to her. My older brother and sister went to bed in their own rooms. My brother escaped into his musical world and my eldest sister into hers of drawing art and working on pictures.

Mom, Leilani, and I read a few chapters of the latest book from J.K. Rowling, "Harry Potter and the Goblet of Fire," before calling it a night. *Our family ritual of reading these stories before bed had been the best part of my childhood. Bonding with my family helped me to relax. When I was younger and couldn't read, mom and Leilani would read, but once I learned to read, I also joined in and we all took turns.*

CHAPTER

I really didn't understand at first. But as the years went by, I thought it was my fault. It was a very confusing time for me.

—Anonymous eighteen-year-old boy

I was not sure When? Why? How? Sometime during the night, I was transported back. I opened my eyes to see grasslands burning before me, Gombi dashed about and a huge squawking creature along with several furry, eerie-looking creatures flying about tried to capture me. I hid behind a tree. As I thought of what to do, I bumped into a rock, which immediately attracted the attention of the creatures directly above my head. Several took a nose dive toward me as I swerved away from one, nearly missed being scraped on the neck by another, and wound up face first in a bush. No time to rest. My palms began to sweat and my heart almost popped out of my chest. Whew, I didn't think I could experience anything like this in my world, but just as I felt a scratch on the end of my nose, I started to fall again.

I laid horizontally and peered up at Soran. He held a feather and waved it voraciously in my face, trying to get me to wake up.

"Hey, stop that, you're tickling me," I demanded.

Standing up and scanning the area to take inventory of the dark and desolate place, the inhabitants that lined the walls watched me. *I feel like I'm missing a bit of time. Last I remember I was only with Soran, but it seems everyone is here now. Not only am I traveling two worlds, I'm time traveling too?* Wormly, Soran, and a few other people gazed into my eyes, so much so that it appeared my soul was being searched.

My eye began doing something weird. I felt as though my eyes were taking over my body, like a possession. I grabbed both sides of my head, trying to gain control of it.

"What is wrong with you all? Why are you staring at me like I'm an alien?"

But no response came, only opened mouths and wide-eyes.

Soran spoke first, "Uh, Josh, your eye, well, it, uh…you didn't feel it?"

Wormly started to explain, "Your eye seems to have a message for us and well, it popped out of your head. Strange really, but I've seen weird things in my lifetime. We're staring because we were trying to decode the cryptic message it was trying to convey," but then he was cut off.

"Just in time," said Pergita, the old wise one.

She seemed to float toward me, while everyone else remained where they were.

"We meet again Joshua. I'm sure you're confused. The spirit of the ancient sacred tree is strong, it's brought you here from your dreams," Pergita said. "Our world is in terrible shape and our homes continue to be destroyed by Gonthragon."

"First off, thank you for saving me, I thought I was done for up there," I motioned above the cabin as she listened. "The spirit, ancient sacred tree? I thought Gonthragon couldn't do any more damage, well for a while anyway. What's new?"

"He's angry from your quick departure and he's sworn to destroy us all if you don't provide him the secret of the Ice Plants. What happened? What made him so angry and why did you just vanish from his throne?" she alternately explained and questioned me.

Target practice had nothing on me, questions kept coming my way, dead center. They wanted answers.

Concentrating on the vision that appeared to me the last time I saw Gonthragon, I explained, "He was questioning me when I was there and after he told me to look into the glasslike orb, well, what I saw was terrible...just terrible and his plans, well...and all I saw...I...I couldn't just stay. He would know the truth if I lied, I'm not good at lying, so I left by the only means I thought would help."

"Our portholes are blocked. How did you do that?" she asked.

"No clue, no idea. Would stabbing my foot cause a block? I thought being in pain would help me get out of there, since it has in the past. Just the sight of him scares me and his foul odor made me gag. He's super creepy and his thoughts, uh, just insane," I said as I used hand gestures to cover my face, throw them up in the air, and cover my head.

"What did he tell you? How do you know of his thoughts?" Pergita asked.

"The orb showed me, I guess, well, it seemed to be a vision...his plan. He has a seriously bad idea for our world if this vision is accurate. His scheme is to annihilate the universe by blowing up this world's core and I cannot, I will not let that ogre do that. I seriously have to get back to mend my family. It's in ruins, but I am needed here too, you know, to save the world?" I said a bit intimidated, but determined.

"The porthole we've been using in our world and the one you've also been using is closed. Gonthragon sealed it. We must travel by way of tea leaves." Soran told the group.

"So the path I've been traveling from my world to yours is your porthole? How did it get closed?" I asked.

"Yes, because something in the prophecy failed. That's the story we've been told anyway," explained Soran.

"I failed in my world. My parents aren't getting back together. I failed miserably." I told everyone. "Could that be why?"

"We aren't sure, but Gonthragon cannot prevent us from moving around worlds using the ancient tea leaves. The spirit is stronger than him," Says Soran.

"Great, I'm not a hero after all! I knew it was only a matter of time before I failed at something in this new world," I complained.

"How do we travel by tea leaves and where do we get those?" I asked.

"Many have been burned, but the Sacred Tree has the special leaves, the ones Gonthragon cannot penetrate or burn. Taking leaves, throwing them, they swirl around and transport you to a place you're thinking of, need, or show you the correct path. It's old magic. Pergita is planting more, but you can tell them apart from others. The veins in the leaves are reversed," she said as she drew one in the dirt.

"Can I travel with them too?" I asked.

"Yes, especially since you were brought here by the spirits." Soran says.

Soran's words replayed in my head again. *It's thought that my failure to reunite my parents was the problem that sealed my fate. I'm doomed if I cannot stop Gonthragon.*

Difficult as it may be, I must gather my strength and devise a way to stop him, keeping my familial problems at bay. I asked Soran to find my journals. I needed the notes I had made to support my efforts. Scurrying ensued as everyone began to organize themselves, giving me the perfect opportunity to think to myself in peace and quiet.

So…Gonthragon has been able to close the portal home and after witnessing the vision earlier in the orb, I now know of his plan, but I'm not quite sure how he is planning to carry this out— oh, shoot, dang it, I forgot, "he" can see and hear my thoughts,

I must gain shelter of the cabin or else he'll gain entry into my mind; I cannot have that now.

Aaahhhhh, no! Are you kidding me? My eye left my head again and then the vision appeared 3-D, right in front of me and I can actually see it.

Gonthragon had assembled his town of Thragons. Remember, they were fire-throwing gargoyle-type birds. They were throwing fire, dousing the entire region with flames, marching around, grabbing Gombi, antlings, Norkels, returning them to be their soldiers. They appeared angry and enraged with squinted eyes and scowls on their faces. Gonthragon was doing the most damage, throwing fire from his mouth and using his claws to grab burning trees and firebombing homes.

Quickly, I peered outside and noticed a bit of gloom as a few of the Norkels had begun to fight each other. Misty wind swirls about as leaves flutter around, intermittently catching on fire.

That's really cool, but super strange at the same time. I wondered how that was happening.

I wondered, is there a connection between the Grasslands? What if Gonthragon's orb is actually HIS eye? He wasn't able to see me when I looked into the orb, but somehow he knew what my plan had been. Can he see into the Norkels' world or anywhere

I traveled here? Does he know of my plan because I viewed his orb with my eye? Hhhmmm, Pergita's words were still whirling through my head. I need to remember. Gonthragon could control the Norkels. He knew what was happening outside the cabins. Well, I recall that I was thinking about my plan, just before I sought cover inside the cabin. How much of my planning did he actually see or could he feel it?

Curious, I called to Pergita. The winds howled and she magically appeared in a rocking-chair. She was older in appearance. Her facial features had increased in the number of wrinkles, she had black and blue circles under her eyes and the expression on her face was like she'd lost every friend she ever had in the world.

"Gonthragon's penetrating this realm, but how? Why is he able to control the Norkels here? What can be done?" my inquisitions ensued of Pergita.

"The only means to stop him are the ancient tea leaves. We used those years ago, but it seems he was closing so many grassland portals and burning tea leaves, which is how we travel and connect with the Sacred Tree. We must reclaim our spirits in the only Sacred Tree and reestablish the portals," she expressed with little hesitation.

She proceeded to explain that he could "see" into our world, but when we moved by way of tea leaves; whether it be through communication or travel, we remained hidden from his view. We both agreed we should continue traveling with tea leaves, until further notice and that cabins were the place to hold meetings and to strategize our attacks. Whilst we discussed this, many Gombi, ant-lings, and other Norkels began assembling into a community room adjoined to her cabin. Soran was planting the remaining tea leaves outside the cabin, on the rooftops and in the door jams; so as to avoid another transport to the grasslands and invasion into our minds.

Heat rushed in as a gust of fire flew through the area surrounding the cabin and our immediate surroundings. It felt like a sauna. I looked around and saw fear in everyone's eyes, even wise Pergita. I saw Soran enter the cabin just in time and he had a handful of the last tea leaves. I had an idea. "Soran, gather as many as you can and transport them with these tea leaves. We must vacate now!"

Moments later I felt my insides gush as my head began to spin like a bowling ball in a tournament. I landed on something sharp and found it to be a Gombi's nose.

"The Sacred Land!" shouted Pergita.

"The what?" I questioned.

Pergita was staring up a tree.

"This is the Sacred Tree. It can only be accessed in times of need and where danger lurks everywhere. We must be in grave danger. We were transported here through the tea leaves," said Pergita.

The skies were baby blue and various shades of greenery surrounded us in the form of trees. They stood like soldiers, protectors. I looked around, Soran, Wormly, and several gombi and antlings were wiping themselves off, walking around and gazing at Pergita.

"Pergita, we need to continue strategizing an attack," I said.

Peering up at the new Sacred Tree, she turned to gaze into my eyes with bewilderment.

"Pergita! The vision in the orb, it's what's going on now, everything burning, lands being wiped out! What can we do if Gonthragon hasn't a weakness? I saw in my vision that I stabbed him with the Ice-Plant spear, but I'm not so sure this will work," I questioned aloud, trying to catch my breath.

"How are you able to see these things?" she questioned me, walking up to me.

"I think it's my eye. It shows me the truth and events that are foretold, but I believe he is also able to see into my mind, which is how he penetrated your realm.

"Interesting…," she said, stroking her head.

Everyone was already looking at me, "He's going to destroy everything and everyone if we don't do something now."

"How can we help?" shouted someone from the crowd.

"I'm thinking," I answered.

I paced back and forth, kicking around tiny pebbles as I walked. *We have to stop him…but how? I know he is after the secret of the Ice-Plants, but what is that? I must get more information about them if I'm going to have any chance.* I joined Pergita and Wormly, who were staring at each other in fear.

"We think we can help you, but it's going to be very dangerous," they said in unison.

"Well, what is it?" I insisted on an answer.

"Where is that ice spear you had when you left for your journeys? This is the ultimate weapon to protect us from Gonthragon, now that the portholes are closed and our only hope of survival," they alternatively spoke, knowing what and when the other was going to start and stop talking. You could tell Wormly and Pergita were in tune with each other.

I searched my pockets and looked around. *Hhhmmm, where was this spear and when did I have it last?* As I pondered, I thought of my family and the fact that I'm going to go to a new school. *Ugh! I visualized my dad with his shoulders hung low, his departure from our house, saddened all the while and then I remembered. The spear was in my dad's suitcase! I thought he would appreciate a memento of me to take with him, so I placed it in his suitcase as a souvenir. Now, he's moved so far away, how will I ever get this back?*

"We have a problem," I said, gesturing with my hand, "and I know where the spear is, uh…it's just that it's not here."

Their bodies almost simultaneously sagged at the reception of my news. Fear was engulfing this place and the mood was very somber.

Pergita spoke up, "You must search your memory very carefully and if you close your eyes, you'll see an image and a location of the spear. It's imperative that you not get distracted or let other thoughts overpower you as so often is the case and why the cabins are burned."

I knew exactly where it was, but to appease the group I did as instructed. I feared they would judge me as so many others do in my world. I couldn't let them down. As I closed my eyes, the vision presented itself and I could see images of my dad and then I saw her. Tall, slender, and wearing a black poncho and a very dark green pointed hat, an evil looking witch! She gazed into my father's eyes as if to put a spell on him. I was enraged! *Okay, okay…this isn't why I'm here, focus your thoughts I told myself, and think about the spear.* Oh yes, there it is, in my dad's green and black plaid suitcase just near the front door.

When I opened my eyes, it was evident that I had let my mind wander and Pergita's warning had become reality as dreadful things happened. A Gombi rushed toward my neck and it was all I could do to escape the cabin.

"Aahhh, I thought you were nice? Why are you attacking me?" I asked the Gombi.

Running to avoid the wrath of the Gombi, all the while wondering what had happened in my *"brief dream-vacation."* I could see I wasn't the only one in trouble. Pergita was tied to a tree with vines and Wormly and Soran were battling other creatures I had never seen before. As soon as I appeared, however, the unknown creatures all vanished and along with them the fearful faces.

"Where did you go?" muttered Pergita. "Did you locate the spear?"

I cannot tell you how confused I was upon my return of being attacked by a Gombi and then having it vanish—voila, as if was never there. Sheesh, what was going on?

"I saw the ice spear, right where I put it in my dad's suitcase, but ugh, I saw someone else. A witch I think!" I said.

Wormly, Soran, and Pergita just looked at each other.

Wormly approached me with a whiplike device and exclaimed, "You'll need this to travel back to your world. It will be a long and dangerous trip. You'll have to travel by way of tea leaves and the Southwinds."

"The what? How can wind be dangerous?" I asked.

"The Southwinds. They are winds that will connect you to the Ancient Sacred Tree," Wormly said.

"How am I going to know if I've found the Southwinds?" I asked already feeling defeated.

Ignoring my question, Wormly continued.

"The only means to take the Southwind is by way of geese, which is why you'll need this whip. It's a type of taming device made of magical potions and Ice Plant extract. You'll be protected from evil invaders and mind intrusions, but you'll always have to have the whip intact with the goose, otherwise you'll be prone to intruders," warned Wormly.

"Huh?" I asked. Used to strange things happening in this world, I went with it.

"Oh, and take this satchel. It's designed to carry the whip and anything else you need, all while remaining almost weightless! Oh, and it has some fruit snacks in it," Soran said.

"Geese, did you say you want me to fly in the wind with geese? And take the, what was it—South-wind?" I inquisitively gestured, all while I shook my head and paced.

"Yes," remarked Wormly and Pergita, both looking haggled and worn with fear in their eyes.

In my world, nobody expected me to be able to get myself dressed and get to school without screwing something up and now this entire world was counting on me. *Oh, no pressure you see, I'm invincible here, but I don't feel it!* Besides, I don't have my medication which helps me focus and calm down, which would definitely come in handy about now.

Wormly and Pergita both told me to take the Southwind. *Did they say fruit snacks? Yum!*

"Again, how do I know when I have found it? How in the world am I going to ride a goose? I'm only five inches tall here. I haven't even seen a goose the whole time I've been here!" I asked question after question, half expecting the answers I received to be concerning.

"To answer your questions, we aren't quite sure exactly where you'll find the geese and the direction of the South-wind is, well…to travel south," they both said in unison.

"You should know, we've never experienced the need to use the geese, since we haven't been in in this situation before, but *"trust your eyes will help you along with the whip itself."* Pergita once felt the presence of a soft, whispering wind, that mentioned feather-decorated creatures that traveled by wind, but only once," they said as they motioned toward the south, where there were plenty of tea leaf trees.

Sighing, as I breathed in and out and looked around I wondered about the day I met Wormly and the look in his eyes. They were counting on *ME! ME!* I wasn't sure why I was chosen for this task and my worst fear was not being success-ful. Doubt encircled my mind just as Pergita placed her hand on my head, tying the whip around it and the tip of my head, she began to chant:

"Oiy ig myah ging cues joynt ig my joi…grant this young lad the courage and protection of the tea leaves and gandering goose which will lead the way on the true path to whatever he seeks," her voice faded as she fell fast into a trance and then…

Pergita continued, "You see, years ago when Gonthragon was just a boy, he was a Norkel, like those here. He was a child that sought truth and justice, similar to you. He lived in an ancient sacred tree and the leaves of that tree were sanctified and full of great spirits of the past. Legend has been told that something happened to change him, something dreadful and painful, but no one or thing knows the truth."

I disentangled the whip from her hand and my head, placed it and my new satchel around my waist, and headed off toward the tea-leaves and South-wind. Half wondering what Pergita's life was like and about my father being brainwashed by this new woman in his life. Either thought wasn't satisfying my need for protection, so I focused on my journey. As I approached the trees, I felt the wind getting mighty blistery.

The sky began to turn black as the sun made its way behind the hills and I forged ahead, on my path to find some geese to aid me in my travels along the South-winds.

It felt like hours had gone by as I continued along my journey, wearing the path beneath my feet. I felt my bones begin to ache from the wind. It was so darn cold. I began to get an eerie feeling, just as before. I searched my surroundings and noticed a tree in the distance. As I approached, out popped this small scaly creature with a spear. I nearly became a shish kabob on the end of it, but was able to dodge its attack, just in the nick of time. Now, normally I would freak out at

THE ANCIENT SACRED TREE: BIRTHING A HERO

this sort of thing, but given the events in my life lately, this I could handle.

"Hey, what's the big idea? What do you want?" I tried to get it to answer me, but it pursued in my direction, not at all friendly.

I got an idea and tried to tie it up with my whip. Dodging and near escapes were how we danced around both each other and the trees, it seemed like hours. Finally, I managed to swing my whip, just perfectly as it became a collar around the neck of this wait, what?

All of a sudden it started to convulse and shake. The body of the creature spun around now…similar to a wind-up toy, but its head remained intact. I was thrown back by the powerful wind produced by the spin and hit my body on a nearby tree. I was shaken, but not unconscious.

My focus was blurry and then as I opened my eyes further, I could see sharply and without distortions. I couldn't believe it. Standing in front of me was a beautiful looking goose! It was beautiful in its appearance, lustrously, smooth ivory feathers, extra long, wispy lashes, and orange webbed feet with a matching beak. I got up. It began to approach me, and I noticed my whip was still entangled around its neck, but had become a crystallized reign of sorts. It bent its head down for me to climb aboard, which was a bit of a challenge being only five inches tall!

I strapped the crystal reign around my waist, place a loop through my satchel, placing its spear inside their too and grabbed the neck of the goose. *Wait, that's my spear. How did he get my spear? Did I drop it? Well, it does work in times of need. Maybe this was one of those times. No clue.*

"Whoah," I said as it began to run at warp speed, which was so fast I couldn't feel the breeze I knew existed as a result. We took flight.

Down below I could see in the distance, dark smoke and fire burning, which I knew was Gonthragon and his evil Thragons at work, destroying the Norkels land. The sky wasn't blue like it was back in my world. It was a deep lavender-blue with beautifully painted white cirrus clouds and swirls of wind, which you could actually see in sky-blue colors.

We were flying and going about our business when my hollow stomach gave rise to my hunger. *Wormly thought of snacks? I need something to eat.* I took out my satchel and, to do so, had to disentangle the whip. I found my dried fruit snacks, which I always took to school and started chewing on them. I realized I hadn't tied the whip back into place, so I immediately reach for the end, which caused me to topple to the side of the goose. I was hanging by only the whip and dangling in midair.

"Aaahhhhh—help me!" but just then I slipped from the whip and down I fell and landed directly on top of a tree. I could hear the goose turning and spinning immediately and knew I would soon be in danger! *Great, I thought—just what I needed now!* The air was chilly and near the edge of a forest of trees. I could see a huge mountain packed with snow. I figured out why it was so cold and thought again about my jacket mom always reminded me to wear. Sure wish I had one now. Burr…the nippiness caused my sweat to form icicles on the tip of my nose. Meanwhile, the goose was no longer a goose, as it reverted back to the scaly creature it was originally and I was fearful for my life as it began to climb the tree, using its spear to make its way closer and closer.

Ahhh, quick think…what shall I do? Okay, calm down. Brrr, it was so cold I thought as my icy brain attempted to devise a plan to get myself out of this mess.

The tree began to shake as if was being cut down by an axe, but just as I look up I was flattened by a sea of snow. It was an avalanche! My heart quickened to prevent my blood from freezing. It all became clear! *The spear, the creature has my spear! I recall when I stabbed my foot, I had done this to escape*

Gonthragon. Why not try it now? I grabbed the spear from the creature, stabbed it into a clump of snow that seemed to be touching my foot and voila, I was back in the land of the Ice Plants. Not the land of the Norkels, but the very entrance to the place in which I found myself days ago, although it was deserted, dark and damp, and smelled a bit of smoke. Relieved to have barely escaped losing my life, my blood began to defrost.

As if my frozen state had prevented me from knowing what to do, immediately I knew exactly what to do. I headed over to the flowering plants, drained the nectar out of one, placed it in my satchel, and dipped the end of the spear inside. The spear became a telescope and I was able to see the location of all my enemies. *Hhhmmm, my eye, it sees the truth and helps me see things others cannot. This must be one of those times. How did I know? I am not sure, I just did. It became a clear vision, just like with the spear.*

Meanwhile, Gonthragon and his dominion were on the outskirts of the burning grasslands, leaving ruins as he torched the area. He was searching and I was sure it was me he was looking for, but in the meantime, I had to find *my* spear, the *magical ice* spear in my dad's suitcase that will help me do away with evil and bring joy and happiness back to this world.

*The spear I have been using is not my magical spear, I have two—
not to confuse you.*

I also saw that most every living creature had been transformed into a Thragon—such a morbid site. Oh my, where
was Pergita and how could I get to my father? Before the
thought could leave my brain, I was being sucked through
what felt like a telescope and came out through the notch of
a tree!

CHAPTER

I hate my sofa. It's where my parents told me they were getting a divorce. I'll never sit on it again.

—Anonymous

I dropped my jaw and threw up my hands, excited to see Pergita, but not really surprised at this point.

"Okay, I'm back at square one. How am I supposed to figure this all out? I'm merely a boy and spirits and sacred leaves are beyond me. Who do you think I am, a magician?" I said throwing my hands up in the air as a sign I'd given up.

Pergita rose and drew a picture in the air. She attempted to explain further. "His ancient sacred tree is between the two realms and can only be reached by you through visions. We aren't quite sure where the location is nor has anyone ventured or dared to journey there. If you go to the ancient tree, you must go alone, but you can take your journal and pen. They are charmed."

"What do you mean charmed?" I was puzzled and scratched my head.

"They work in conjunction with your eyes, but you are the only one that can control them, as legend tells it," Pergita explained.

Hhhmmm…what could have happened to him in this realm to have made this task so secretive? It's just a mystery. I know I'm the seeker of truth and justice and my visions, seen through my magical eye, are a key to finding the Ancient Sacred Tree. My emotions are also connected to this realm, as I was not angry or depressed here. Pergita seemed to remotely explain all this to me, and although intrigued, I was not for certain why the story could be told so matter-of-factly, as she was telling it to me now. My interest was piqued and as with the passing of each minute, I become more curious.

"Joshua, do you feel you're up for the task," uttered Wormly. The first response I'd heard from him for quite some time. I also was not cognizant of his presence the whole time.

"Surely it's a lot to process and I'm still trying to make sense of everything, especially what I've just learned today. Me, they were counting on me to travel by tea leaves or goose, to track Gonthragon, who used to be a Norkel, but something bad happened to him. I know that pain caused me to travel in and out of worlds, sometimes my own, but lately only throughout this world. I sense eerie things before they happen and I believe my eye is the connection, through the visions I can only see. I'm supposed to travel and see something about Gonthragon's plan to stop him. I'm still not quite sure how, but I was already on my journey and now had been brought back to my starting point. How much time do I have to resolve this? Just curious if time is also going to be working against me," I questioned, placing my right hand on my head, raising my left, palm up, an expression of a thinker.

"There is a magical map within the pages of your journal. The time it will be revealed is the time in which you'll need it," Wormy mentioned.

"Great, now you tell me this?" I asked.

"Like with all your tools and information along this journey it's available when needed," Wormly states.

"So let me get this straight. I'm going to use a map to get to an unknown place, but I'm not going to see it until it's revealed?" I asked.

"Precisely! You are correct!" Wormly said as his face lit up.

"Perfect!" I sarcastically replied.

Just then Soran came over and knocked my journal I was incidentally just viewing out of my hands. He proceeded to crawl over it as steam began to rise from within the pages of my journal. Hot liquid, the color of tea, flowed from within the middle of the journal as the pages spilled open. We all climbed on top of Ice Plant slides to avoid being drenched by the liquid. Pergita waved her hands and my pen magically flowed through the air, ever so slowly, swirling and seemingly becoming a type of "stir-stick," The liquid swirled and the pages become broken tea bags as we all stared in amazement at the sight before us.

Lickety-split, the liquid, tea bags, and stir-stick spun around and disappeared with a flash. What was left behind was a pile of wet "tea leaves," my book, pen, and a map.

I stood up and immediately and began clapping, "Whoa, what an awesome trick, do that again!" I ordered, similar to a kid seeing his first magic trick.

"Uh, that wasn't me," said Wormly.

"Nor me," said Pergita.

"What do you mean, then who did that?" I insisted they answer. "Soran?"

"Perhaps it was you," they said in unison.

Lacking indication of how or what just happened, it appeared to have been some type of magic or amazing trick. Both my journal and pen looked unharmed and untouched. The whole of the area one would expect to be wet or full of puddles of water left behind was completely dry. Well, except for the tea leaves.

I wasn't quite sure I was up to the task of finding the Ancient Sacred Tree, fixing the portholes and destroying Gonthragon, but I instantly remembered my family and I knew I needed to get back there soon. I imagined my dad, sisters, and brother, and mom, who were always at the forefront of my mind.

Knowing that I could not return to my land, until I defeated this evil Gonthragon, I gained strength. I also couldn't fathom what dreadful thing could have altered the life of a young Norkel, such as Gonthragon, if that was even his name as a boy.

The task was mine to tackle and the news today had surely been helpful. But I hadn't a clue where to begin the journey. Instantly, just as soon as I thought this, I remembered, "There's a map! A map! Yes, of course," I said to myself.

My eyes focused and my attention was drawn to Pergita and Wormly who seemed confused. Both were staring at the map and arguing about where the Ancient Sacred Tree could be found. The interesting thing was they both seemed to be looking at a different map as I could ascertain by the way they were describing items on the map.

"Joshua, come over here and let us know if you can see the tree on our map," Wormly gestured.

As I walked over, I could see part of the map, which appeared to be blank. I looked at it and suddenly, as if by magic, a portion of the map started to draw itself. First, I saw what looked to be me, then an image of Wormly, followed by Pergita. The only image other than ourselves was that of the cabin with a door and a small little trail. As I stood up with the map in my hand, I walked to the door. Each step I took, the map began to fill in and led me down the path as I walked.

"Hhhmmm," I uttered a response, "I don't believe either of you see the map as I see it! Mine was incomplete and only continued to fill in as I traveled and followed the path, interesting map!" I exclaimed.

"Bye, I'm off then," I said and waved to them.

They both looked eerily at each other and then waved goodbye to me as I followed the map to complete my task at hand, find the Ancient Sacred Tree, and restore the portals, preventing Gonthragon from completely destroying all realms.

CHAPTER

I'm always dreaming of my parents dying. They drink poison and scream for help. I can't get through the door to help them. It's my fault they die. I want to take poison and die too.

—Anonymous

I began the journey of finding the Ancient Sacred Tree and thereby the tea leaves, but I knew that I mustn't confer this knowledge with anyone. Revealing any component of this fact to outsiders could create a new portal for Gonthragon and his army to enter the Norkel realm and completely destroy all regions of their realm. I grasped my journal and pen in hand, decisively inspecting the pen, I realized that there was a small object embedded within the handle. Upon deeper analysis, I saw there was a tube of clear mystically luminescent liquid inside with an ancient scroll-like paper inside a smaller tube in the handle I unrolled it. I read it:

Ice Plant ink, the secret to controlling all and future realms. Created by Shaman, to be used with extreme caution.

I immediately felt a sense of grief and sadness as if something had overtaken my body. *Oh no I thought.* Then suddenly a loud thwack and I was immediately thrown toward a humongous door or what appeared to be as I felt a handle on it, which somehow appeared from thin air. I could hear the sounds of what seemed to be wolves howling. I couldn't quite see. It was entirely black…I began to breathe profusely, my lungs pulsating as if they were going to explode as my chest rose and collapsed without hesitation. The ground where I stood gave way, simultaneously as I felt a sharp object, perhaps a claw, reached out and scratched my arm.

"Ouch," I screamed. "Damn, that really hurt…"

I felt softness beneath me and then a slap across my face and the lights were on!

"What the hell…Leilani? Is that you? How? What? WWWWhere? Oh my gosh, why did you slap me? Damn it, Leilani, you slapped me, but I'm so happy to see you! I just saw you in a vision I had, while I was falling and then I was scratched, but I'm not sure how or by what. Wait a minute, where are we? We aren't in Hayward, are we? Where's mom? Where's dad? Where did you come from? What, what, what?" I demanded answers.

She slapped me again and then again, "Dad came to pick us up"—slap—"but you didn't want to go"—slap—"so he took me instead," she said, then punched me in the stomach.

I grabbed my stomach, touched my face, and stared at my arm.

"Damn Leilani, I'm already hurting, what's going on?" I insisted she answer my questions and was going to continue to ask her until she did.

"I'm not sure, you're the one with all the answers and constant ramblings about your adventures. You tell me!" she demanded.

"I haven't a clue. I was battling and then all of a sudden you appeared…oh yeah, and slapped me!"

"Well, I don't know where to start and well, this may be a bit of a shock to you…but here goes. Dad's getting married again and—" she was cut off.

"He already told us he's getting married, what—" I was cut off.

"Josh listen, she's not very nice, in fact, she's quite evil. When I met her, I sensed something about her, but I couldn't quite figure it out. I just don't trust her," she spoke as she gazed at my arm.

"You really don't know what happened to your arm? Where have you been this whole time, I've been worried about you, so has mom. She's been really crying. She won't let anyone search for you. She insists you'll return soon and that this isn't the first time you've run away," she explained. "Remember that time when you were gone all day, we found you in a vacant lot with a stick, waving it around like you were a superhero or wizard?" Leilani brought up an event from our past.

"Yes, I remember, but this isn't the same—" she cut me off.

"Mom was so relieved to see you, but mad you left home and wandered off. You were upset when you didn't get to finish your story at school and she thought you were in the yard still, remember?" she coached me.

"Ran away? Why on earth does she think I've run away?" I emphatically responded to her bit of news. My head was really aching now and my arm was throbbing as I sat down to give my lungs a chance to catch up to my breathing and tried to rationalize all that had transpired. Besides, my stomach and face are still red from where my sister caused me pain! *Did mom really think I ran away? I wouldn't.*

"Mom can't think that. I promised mom I wouldn't run away again, I swore. I guess, well, I can't help it sometimes, it just happens," I apologetically said to my sister.

The vision: Oh what is this feeling? I'm so sad, what is going on? I picked myself up off the ground and in the distance I could see a house where smoke was emitting from the chimney and Redwoods encircled its place. I can hear voices, but they are so faint, I cannot hear very well. I decided to take a closer look. As I approached the window, I could hear the voice of my dad.

"You don't know where he is, but he's been gone for three days? Did you call the police? Maybe he ran away or something terrifying has happened to him," he said into the phone.

What? Could he be talking about me? I've been gone that long? It hadn't felt like that long, but I was stuck for a bit. Trapped was more like it.

"Darling, do you have to have those children over this weekend?" I could hear another not so friendly female voice say.

My father just scratched his head and paced the floor, not quite sure what to do. Just then I noticed Leilani being dropped off by our aunt. She walked up to the door, knocked and my dad opened it.

"Leilani, how did you get here?" my dad questioned. I could tell by the expression on my soon to be stepmother's face she wasn't happy with this. My sister walked in, and my dad closed the door. I thought to myself that I had to get their attention, and I must get that spear. Oh boy, what would my dad think if he saw me?

Present.

So the last I remembered, I was on my journey and I had to travel and find the Ancient Sacred Tree. I had my journal, my pen, and my map. My map, where was my map? I scanned the room, looking for signs of those items necessary for my journey. My journal was upside down on top of the bunk bed, and my pen was lodged in the closet door, similar to the *Sword in the Stone*, an old Disney movie. My map, where was my map? I examined the atrocious scene my abrupt arrival had caused, all the while searching for my map. The air was damp and the walls were lined with bookshelves and stuffed animals, which were torn to pieces now and lying all over the beige-carpeted floors. The bunk bed, which appeared to have been ornately decorated with carvings of gargoyles and other ancient figurines, was now a pile of wood, feathers, and fabric on the floor. As I rose, I brushed myself off, ignoring my throbbing arm and turned to my sister.

"Have you seen a large piece of parchment paper?" I asked, looking quizzically as I scanned the room.

"You mean this," my sister said as she waved my map into the air as if she wanted me to chase her for it.

"Give me that, it's really important!" I said, disgruntled.

I lurched forward, trying to get it out of her hands without ripping it at the same time. I twisted my body to also pick up the journal and dislodged the pen from where it was anchored. Just as I touched the edge of the map, I felt the floor vanish, and the similar hollow feeling in my body that I felt just moments ago returned. I grappled with the items, attempting to secure them in my clutches while trying to ascertain the tickling in my ear. I felt as though someone or something was piggy-backed on me.

"What's happening!" shouts a familiar voice.

We landed at the edge of a cliff occupied by a large tree, which shades and protects us from the external movements and visitors. The latter was more likely as I sensed eyes upon this place. I glanced around—*map, pen, journal*—okay, all my possessions were accounted for as I used what was left of my stamina to stand.

"Are you okay?" I asked Leilani just before she slapped me in the face. By this time, I must have a bruise on my face from all of my sister's slaps. She sure knows how to make me feel welcomed and loved. I recalled all the moments in our house when she barged into my room and jumped on top of my bed. Usually she was punching me in the stomach. Slapping was a new punishment she was dishing out to me.

"Uh, what the heck, what just happened? Where the hell are we, and why are you so worried about that map?" she managed to muster a seemingly irritated yet worried response.

I found myself in a bit of a predicament having to explain everything that had happened to me since I fell into the Ice Plants, my eye, Gonthragon, the visions, and what they all meant. She sat and listened with her legs bent in a crouched position, her arms wrapped around her legs, her chin rested on her knees and her big brown eyes gazed into mine. Her hair was long dark chocolate with curls that cascaded down her

Cherokee cheekbones. The freckles on her face highlighted her beauty and as I spoke, she listened. She did not chastise me or interrupt the story (which was surprising for her) that I ultimately had to dispel to her. Eerily, she just sat there soaking it all in.

The moment was uneventful with the exception of my sister's eyes, which were full of tears. I just finished explaining that I wasn't sure what injured my arm and she rose, lifted me up, and just held me tight. Our embrace seemed to be an eternity and then she spoke.

"You think we're stuck here? Oh my gosh, what are we going to do? Josh, if anyone can find the Ancient Sacred Tree it's you! I know you and exploration is something you are skilled at doing. You've been born to do this. Remember when we used to play CSI in your room? We worked well together, perhaps it was all practice for this day now? Besides, two heads are better than one, in most cases, so what can I do to help?" she insisted.

"There's something about this map and its connection to me," I thought out loud.

"Yeah, I know since I cannot see a thing on it, but tarnished parchment," Leilani interrupted.

"Right, and when I was looking at it with Pergita and Wormly, they both saw different things and just before I found you, well uh, I thought it would be nice if you were here with me, like old times. That's when I landed, uh…in that room," I explained.

"Dad is going to be really worried," she stopped me.

"I don't think so, after all he's getting married and has moved far away from us. He's not thinking of us. He's replacing us with a new family! You know he doesn't care about us, right?" I irritatingly responded to her statement.

"Stop doing that, you know he does care and he'll be worried. He's probably trying to find us now," she defended our dad.

I glanced over at my tools and wondered if this journey was worth it or not. I mean how can I deal with separating from my family, and a divorce, and a new marriage, all while fixing the problems with this world and the other many realms? I didn't sign up for this, and I didn't think it was fair that I was pressured with so much responsibility.

Just then I noticed the map, it had changed and my pen was scribbling a picture, an image, no, wait—not an image but an entryway, what? What was this? Uh, my gosh, it was, it was my dad. What in the world was going on? I peered over at Leilani. She was oblivious to this image and awaited my response, deeply affected by it as was evident by the increase in tears around her eyes.

"Leilani, hurry, hold my hand," I ordered, and immediately I picked up the map, tugged my sister's hand and off we went. This time, I felt we were riding on a slide, twisting, and turning in every direction. The walls of this place were lined with moss, leaves, and intermittent waterfalls. It reminded me of Maui and I told Leilani to open her eyes.

"Huh, what do you mean?" she closed her eyes, just as quickly as she had opened them.

The vision now was from the topmost slope of a slide, you know when you're staring down the edge of a slide, searching and waiting for someone there at the end to catch you? Well, this someone happened to be my father. I was so confused. He hadn't done this since I was little at the Pepsi Park.

But just as quickly as this vision appeared, it disappeared. We were both face down on the ground, after a soft landing and my father was staring quizzically at us both.

"Dad? Oh my gosh…what are you doing here?" I inquired of him.

"Uh, what just happened? Where did you two come from? What the heck? Are you impostors? Where are my kids?" my dad questioned.

"Dad, it's us and we have something to tell you," we said in unison.

My dad looked really confused as he walked over to both of us, inspecting our faces, touching our skin, peering deeply into our eyes. Then, without any other sign of confusion he continued.

"Josh, my man, where have you been? You've worried both your mother and I and we have been searching everywhere for you! Leilani even came to the house helping us search," my dad explained, "but then she disappeared and now the two of you are here?"

"Dad? That's all you have to say to me, I've been through so much, but that's okay, nice to see you too," I replied a bit irritated. *After all, doesn't he know that I'm hurting because of the divorce and Leilani said he was worried, but all he does now is blame me for not being there. Well, I could do the same of him.*

Trembling inside, *what am I going to do? This map isn't working.* The map kept taking me to people I'm worried about and to places I had never seen. I was supposed to find the Ancient Sacred Tree, yet I kept finding my family. I wondered why and how was I going to get to where I needed to go? I thought about the moment Pergita and Wormly were telling me of my task. I know my success was connected to me and my thoughts, but I kept getting distracted by my personal feelings. Ugh, I'll never find the tree and I'll be trapped here forever, we all will.

I walked over to my dad, "I'm sorry, I didn't mean that, I'm just really worried, that's all," I said facing my dad.

"It's okay man, I understand. I get that way too and I shouldn't have yelled, but I was really and truly worried and your mother has been beside herself with worry. She was searching through your things in your room and found one of your journals you were writing in this past year. She said you were quite angry, which was apparent through the dreams you wrote about. You know, I used to have very upsetting and vivid dreams too, when I was younger? I used to dream about a far off land and I used to travel there in my dreams, you know, like Peter Pan in Neverland? Anyway, I met some strange creatures and it seemed so real, but yet I always woke up in my room. The dreams used to be something I had ritually every night, but the day you went to the hospital to have eye surgery, well, they stopped. I haven't had another dream.

I can't even remember dreaming," my dad spilled out his feelings to me.

"Dad, you've never mentioned this before? Do you know what I have been through lately? Why haven't you ever told us of these dreams?" I demanded of my dad.

"I'm not sure why I haven't told you, let alone anyone about these dreams. I do know that I was told my dreams were to be kept secret. The creature that controlled my dreams told me, actually, it wasn't a creature, but a very nice older spirit. I never knew who or what, just a narrated voice in my dream. I feel a sense of calm now, as if I'm supposed to reveal this to you now, is that peculiar?" my dad responded inquisitively.

"Hhmm, yes a bit curious, but quite plausible and I speculate the bizarre events we've experienced here are connected to your dreams and my ventures," I explained to them both.

Now, our only recourse was to find the Ancient Sacred Tree and gather the only remaining tea leaves. They were our only means of communicating to other realms, stopping Gonthragon and getting back to Hayward.

"Leilani, dad, we have to follow my map, —but first, tell dad all I told you, I have to examine this map further using my pen," I advised them both.

As Leilani filled dad in on all that had happened, I tried to figure out how my energy can control the map and not the other way around. The scroll mentioned the ink controls other realms, but I only wanted to find the Ancient Sacred Tree, oh and I needed the spear. Just then my dad handed me the spear, then told me this was the reason I was in his vision. I was perplexed by this news and how he knew, but then thought about the ink and my map. *Hhhhmmm, maybe I could use it to find a doorway to the tree.* Perhaps if I placed the ink on the end of the pen and as I did this…the map came alive with images from the ink in my pen, then I blacked out.

11

CHAPTER

Heat enveloped the immediate surroundings, and I couldn't quite tell where Dad, Leilani, and I were, but heard squawking sounds that sounded similar and my shoulder throbbed with an unbearable pain. Those horrible gargoyles were over our heads and we had to run and duck to avoid them. Dad just stared in a trance. He didn't move. "Dad!" I screamed, just as I jumped in between him and a gargoyle that was nose-diving and just before I got there, attempted to peck out his eyes.

Leilani was crouched behind a boulder, her hands hurriedly trying to cover her head, which was where I shoved dad. We all were out of their reach and I thought the narrow spaces between the huge boulders were a safe haven for us from the gargoyles. I couldn't be more wrong as I stepped backward, the rear entry to our hiding place had a wide opening and I felt a familiar claw. Next thing I knew we were all screaming again, being carried away by the creepy flying creatures. The underside of my pilot had a foul odor and an obnoxious feeling overtook me. I began to feel queasy.

"Aaaahhhhh, help me, Josh!" screamed Leilani.

"Josh, we are going to be okay, concentrate on helping us, don't panic!" warned Dad, finally out of his trance.

We were all being dragged to what I felt would be our doom if I just did nothing. Remembering my vision in the throne room I got an idea. My spear was still in my hand, but I couldn't get a good grasp to use it. Thoughts were filling my mind and I contrived a plan. My only hope was that we were going to the same place otherwise, my plan would fail to save us all.

Just then I could feel my pilot slowing down and saw a window up ahead. It seemed familiar, although I couldn't really remember where I had seen it before. I ensured to hold my spear tightly when the creature flung me into the open window. I spun on the floor and stopped with my head under my body, my legs bent backward, and my spear tumbled across the floor. Just as I feared, my father and sister were nowhere in sight and I was alone.

The room was misty and the walls were crawling. I had been here before. The monster met me here. It was Gonthragon's chamber, where I left him at his throne. My head hurt and my body temperature was rising again.

This chamber had no doors that I could see and the only entrance was the hole in the wall from where I entered, I called a window. I stared outside and as far as I could see, there were grasslands. Far in the distance I could see smoke. Is *that where Gonthragon attacked us? Is the smoke from the Norkels' land in Green Burough Valley and the Ice Plants?* I felt my pockets for my possessions, I only had my journal and just as I looked up to locate my spear, a figure appeared and it spoke to me.

"Hello, my name is Selia, and I'm going to get you some food. I hope you aren't afraid of me, I'm not the enemy, remember that, okay?" she spoke.

"Well, hello, I'm…"

"I know who you are and I've been searching for you for quite some time now, but later for that. We cannot talk here, it's too dangerous, I'll send someone for you later," she whispered.

I could hear squawking and in came the same foul-smelling gargoyle that carried or should I say threw me into this place. He appeared and began charging in my direction. Just as he neared my head, he turned around, exited through the window and took flight.

This place is teeming with really weird creatures and events. I must find Leilani and dad. Where would they have been taken? If only I had my map I'm sure I could imagine a route to them or an escape route for us all to get out. Wormly and Soran must be worried and dad and Leilani haven't a clue how to get around in this world. I'm no William Clark, but I have been in this world a tad longer and I'm destined to save the Norkels. I'm determined to be victorious in my efforts and according to the book I read about Galileo, he was also determined.

Just as I started thinking again, Selia came in with some food and a drink. "I have an idea where your family is and I'll help you get to them. I hear they have your map from the Norkels, is that true?" she inquired of me.

I'm not quite sure I should trust her, but what choice do I have in here? She did make the comment that I should trust her, but I've also been told not to trust anyone.

"My map was lost in flight, maybe the gargoyles have it, I'm not quite sure," I lied.

Selia stepped closer; she was in the dark, so her appearance hadn't been very clear to me. Her hair was deep black and slightly curly, but one could not quite distinguish this, as she kept her hair tied up. My eye was a bit magical. It helped me *see* these things. She appeared to be a cross between a homeless person and a beggar. Her clothes were tattered and soiled and she appeared and smelled as though she hadn't bathed in weeks. "You must be moved, so eat quickly, we haven't much time." She gestured toward what I just notice for the first time as a door. *Hmm, where did that come from? Weird!*

The gargoyle that exited through the window appeared once again. He grabbed a handful of worms from the moving ceiling, and popped them into his mouth. Cringing at the grotesque sight and sound of it ingesting the grub from the room, I realize it standing next to me.

"He's joining us," was all Selia said.

I stared at Selia. She stared back, but I could not ascertain her mood, thoughts, or plan.

Selia, the gargoyle, and I headed toward the hallway and I was continuously poked in the back, a sign to move it along I presumed.

The corridor was damp, pitch black, and I tried to remember the journey for future reference. We turned left, then left again, and there was a bit of flickering light as if from a candle ahead. The path narrowed and we descended some stairs that seemed to curve to the right. Sporadically, light shined from antique, rusty old lamps in the shape of gargoyles. I stared straight ahead, but the lamps seemed to be alive, just like the walls in the other part of this chamber. Fire escaped the mouths of the lamps and lit our path. Once we reached the bottom of the staircase, all flickering light subsided and it was the darkest black. Scuffling ensued and I felt a pull and tug off to the left. I was blindfolded by something cloth-like, but why I was not sure as I could not see a thing. I heard a loud scruffy holler and was immediately shoved into what felt like a doorway.

CHAPTER

The blindfold was removed, allowing me to clearly see my dad and Leilani. Both stared at me. "W-w-what? W-w-Where did you go? Oh my gosh, I thought we were done for…but I'm glad you're alive," I said to them both, grabbing and hugging them.

"Well, Leilani and I were separated at first and I was in this dark place," my dad revealed to us. "I heard someone whisper 'everything will be fine, she's coming' and then I could feel someone tugging on my arm. Leilani took me into a cabin. It was lit and we met a woman named Pergita. She was the voice and then we showed up here," my dad blurted out as if he just couldn't wait to tell the story.

"You met Pergita? What did she say? Was she alone?" I sounded like I was probing them for answers, which I was.

"Yes, we did," Leilani answered "and she was quite nice, but only whispered that we should return."

"That was probably the cabin where I met her and began my journey, which I still need to finish. We have to be on our way. We have to make it to the Ancient Sacred Tree. We need to find the map first," I reminded them.

"The map is with me," Leilani exclaimed. "You said it was important and I saw it in action with you, so when the gargoyle captured us, I tucked it away in my bag. Here!"

"Oh Leilani, you've saved the day!" I told her, throwing my arms around her.

Relieved to have my map back, now my journey, our journey, could continue. I scanned my map. It began drawing a picture of a tree, but wait…not only a tree, a forest, uh…a forest with thousands upon thousands of trees. Next, the map drew mountains and valleys and more trees! *How can I find the Ancient Sacred Tree through the many thousands that lay before me on this map? What can I do? How am I to get there?* Just then, the map started drawing snow. *Oh yeah, make it snow. That's just great, I hate the snow. I'm moody in the snow and it's dark when there's no sun. I'm feeling a bit defeated right now and I'm not quite sure I can live up to this adventure, no this daunting task that lay before me. I'm only eight, a hero maybe, that's what Wormly said, but THIS, nobody said anything about traveling through snowy mountains and being on the lookout for ONE Ancient Sacred Tree when so many surrounded it. Oh, I'm so out of my league here!*

"You'll never believe it, but the map has revealed the area where the Ancient Sacred Tree can be found. Only trouble is, there's millions of trees and mountains and snow. Guys, I'm not so sure I'm up for this adventure or quite cut out for this," I admitted, shrugging my shoulders as I let my hand that held the map collapse to my side and I stared at my feet.

"Josh, you are meant for this journey. You've been practicing for this your whole life in our backyard. I know you've enough strength and courage. You mustn't give into your fears or doubts!" Leilani advised me as she walked over to our dad and nudged him.

"Josh my man, you're really gifted and use a spear like nobody I've seen before. The journey seems like it's rather a difficult one, but you've tackled so many obstacles in your way, right? You can do this, we both have faith in you and God wouldn't put you in this situation if you couldn't handle it," my dad responded and he walked over and put a hand on my shoulder.

"Okay, I'm not quite sure of this, but you all seem to have faith in me, I can't let you down. Selia, the map has revealed a journey that I must travel and I'm not prepared with essentials of traveling in the snow. Do you have anything I can take along with me?" I inquired.

Selia walked out of the door down the hall, only to return and stare at us all.

"Well, are you coming?" she questioned.

We all followed her down a hallway and into another room, which was extremely cold, but the walls were still alive with movement. I felt like I was in my mom's freezer. My teeth began to chatter around in my mouth and it was hard to contain them. As suddenly as we entered the cold, we left it and just "appeared" in another room.

"Whoa, how did you do that," we all said in unison.

Of course my teeth weren't chattering anymore and I was staring at the walls. They weren't moving.

"Selia, how did you do that? Are we still in Gonthragon's castle? What was that, some kind of portal?" I inquired, "I thought those were closed."

"Joshua, you have been destined for this journey for quite some time. Designated as your personal tour guide, it's a pleasure to serve you and this room is yours. We have a selection of items that have been taken from various realms, leaders, and Shaman over the years, all stashed in this room. Some of them are enchanted and will only act on your instructions. The only person to gain entrance to this is you, your eyes are the only ones. You have a magical eye, one you received when you were very young, yes?"

"Yeah...," I said.

"Well, this was no accident. Please, please, do step up and look into this port," Selia gestured as I approached her.

Stepping up to the port required little effort and as I did this, and if by magic, a door appeared and we were allowed to enter. The room was like no other I'd seen before, lined with golden-carved leaves, similar to the ones on the carriage that took me on my first journey. Inlaid between the leaves were mirrors making the whole room appear larger in size. I stepped in to gain a closer look at the room. Parcels and packages were nicely stacked in rows, marked on the front of each row with a label marked in black pen, but the font seemed to be in some type of calligraphy. I was quite impressed and continued to inspect the various corners and items that were garnered in the room for my journey.

My dad and Leilani began to search each parcel in the room and awed at the sight before us, but nothing quite astonished me more than the thing that happened next.

Suddenly, stars and fireworks began appearing, simultaneously throughout eighteen of the rows of objects like packages and boxes, about every other row. They seemed to each be coming from a package or parcel. I looked at Selia and she ushered me to the nearest one.

"It's a sign. You must search inside this package to find an item for your journey. You will know which one to take," she said moving away to let me in closer.

The first box that I approached stopped sparking as I opened the top, and I was hesitant to get near, not sure what was inside. Box flaps needed to be pulled back, and at first, I didn't see anything. I had to get closer to it and stared directly inside the box. Another vision:

I'm climbing up a huge mountain, and it's quite steep. I see my foot seem to slip, and quickly I reached into my satchel and pulled out a rope. My rope is fairly short, only a foot, but when I throw it out, it lengthened and wrapped around a tree at the top of the mountain. I used the rope to pull myself up.

The vision disappeared as suddenly as it appeared and left inside the box was a rope. I couldn't help but think the vision was what I'm expected to face on the mountain, so I grabbed the rope and continued to the next box with fireworks exploding out of the top.

After collecting the next five items, my collection contained an ice spear, a warm fur-lined jacket, fire-starter, quick water, transforming hiking boots that can included walking tennis rackets, given weather conditions, and a rope. I was well equipped for my journey, however, I was not sure how or what I'm supposed to gain nourishment from. As if on cue, Selia walked up to me with a plate of circular disks, she called them "Power Disks."

"When you're hungry, find shelter and place one of these on your tongue. You'll be amazed at what happens," she exclaimed.

I took one off the plate, as did everyone else and I placed it on my tongue. Nothing happened!

"Is this some kind of trick? What is this Selia?" I inquire of her.

"Oh, almost forgot. When you're on your journey, you use it after you have found shelter. We aren't on your journey, so you'll have to imagine your favorite meal," she said a little embarrassed and blushed.

We all did this and to my surprise I began to taste the following: juicy ham hocks, creamy macaroni and cheese, and then jelly beans for dessert. I couldn't believe how real the flavors were in my mouth. My stomach had expanded since tasting the Power Disks and I'm literally full too. I needed that. I hadn't eaten for quite a while.

Well, it appeared that I'm ready! I am equipped, I have my items, my spear, my map, and food. What more do I need for my journey? Well, a companion would be nice!

"Who is going with me?"

Leilani said she was up for a venture, but Selia stated she was supposed to travel with me as a guiding star.

"You see Joshua, I'm a secret weapon that Gonthragon hasn't been aware of since he found me. I've been living here homeless in the back part of the chambers. Now, you are truly here to live out your destiny, saving the Norkels and all who live in their land. It's been prophesied for years. Your father here needs to make a trip to the Shaman. He is also destined to complete that circle that began with his grandfather. Your sister must remain behind, just in case your mother is able to break through, also part of the prophecy," she paused.

"My mother, in the prophecy? Oh, I bet she'd love that one. She would kill any evil doer. Have you seen her drive? She's scary, even my friends are fearful of her. Anyway, how is she supposed to know about the prophecy? What if Gonthragon finds Leilani, what then?" I was really curious and worried about my family. I needed answers.

"You need not worry. All will be taken care of here, and I'm leaving Leilani in the trusted hands of my friend, Snoob."

CHAPTER

aying goodbye sucks. *I wish the world was safe, calm, and everyone could just live in peace.* Obligation and the necessity of ending this prophecy had taken over my emotion. My family and this world must be saved.

My father was well on his way to completing his part in fulfilling the prophecy and Leilani was busy making friends with Snoob. I grabbed my map, packed my satchel with my rope, spear, ice spear, Power Disks, fire-starter and quick-water slipped on my jacket, put on my satchel, tied my hiking boots and off I went. *Haha, I feel like Indiana Jones, maybe I look like him too.*

The only means of even knowing where to begin was with the map. It was in my hand. *Stare at it, that's how it works.*

As I stared at the map, I felt my eye as it swirled around. I closed them both, and as I did so, the icy air whistled around my face, swished my hair, and my face numbed by its sting. Determined to find the Ancient Sacred Tree, I concentrated harder. *Selia said my map would work if I'm on my journey. I am, but nothing is happening! What's going on?* Focused, I sat on a rock and waited for the reveal.

I opened my eyes and noticed a brilliant white dust all over the map. The trees were dusted with snowflakes and the mountains were covered in snow.

"Okay, Selia, I think I know the way!" I said as I got up to begin my journey.

Selia didn't respond and I turned around to make sure she hadn't vanished and noticed she attached herself to my jacket hood.

"I didn't know you were magic too? How'd you get so small?" I said to a bug-size Selia.

"Sshhh, we mustn't draw attention to ourselves," was all she said.

Leaving fresh, crisp footprints in the snow behind me, I focused on my journey and continued in pursuit of the Ancient Sacred Tree.

Snow began to fall slowly and gently brushed my face tickling my nose. I stuck out my tongue to have a taste. The flakes reminded me of snow cones, minus the flavored syrup of course.

Peaceful solitude was something I enjoyed and it was quiet, too quiet. My jacket also felt a little light, so I rotated my head around and noticed Selia sat in the snow.

"What are you doing?" I whispered.

I walked over to her, stuck out my hand and helped her onto her feet.

"Why are you stopping?" I asked her.

"Joshua, we have a long journey in front of us and you must be very alert. Look around, we are not alone, even though it appears isolated. You have to be ready for anything out here," she insisted looking into my eyes.

"Selia, I am grateful you came with me, I hate being alone. I'm always alone and it's depressing. This snow and cold weather doesn't help me any, so having a friend is a relief. Keeping my eyes and ears open is my plan, along with keeping us alive," I said.

"So long as you're prepared, I can walk alongside you," she responded.

Whilst Selia arose, her whole body appeared to shake and instantly became life-size again.

Both of us left footprints in the snow as we walked and a memory filtered through my mind of a picture my mom had of footprints in the sand. I hope neither one of us has to carry the other.

Directly in front of us was a fork in the road, one path was uphill, one seemed to flow between two mountains.

"I'm not quite certain that the Ancient Sacred Tree is higher than we are currently traveling, but I believe we should be heading up a mountain. This road could be the best option," I said.

Selia just stared at me.

"A snow storm could begin, however, and we could get stuck, so taking the low road between two mountains through a valley isn't a poor option either. Selia, which way should we go?" I asked her.

"Joshua, you are the one with the map and the 'chosen one,' so to speak. I'm only here as a spiritual guidance, someone to support you in time of *need*. You must make this choice. Analyze your options," Selia said, which was no help to me.

As I glanced at the map, I noticed a small flickering on the road leading between the mountains. It was a sign. Off we went, following the low road.

The scenery was beautiful, quiet and peaceful, although it snowed and my body felt like a Popsicle. Wispy flakes of snow frosted the trees, rocks, and everything within our sight was white. The river, or what I presumed by twisted curves embedded in the snow, was icy and frosted over.

Serene and peaceful had been our journey for about thirty minutes, until I noticed something along the path up ahead. Approaching the path, it appeared the snow level was jagged directly in front of us about one hundred and twenty yards ahead. Selia and I glanced at each other, both our faces looking quizzically. The snow had stopped at this point and the hair on my whole body seemed to be standing on end. Reminded of Selia's cautionary words, I proceeded carefully.

I stood directly over the hole in the path and the changed snow level we witnessed earlier must have been the snow from which this hole was made. It was full of water. I scanned the area and it appeared we were walking on a path made by snow and ice accumulating over the lake. I'm not quite sure how large it was. Nevertheless, the water was murky and calm.

"This hole is fresh," I said.

"Joshua, look out," she screamed.

Something crawled onto my pant leg and with so many clothes on, I couldn't feel it. I started shaking my leg but the harder I shook, the tighter it clung. It wasn't letting go. Panicking, which wasn't good for my anxiety, I turned to Selia again, she was gone.

"Selia, where are you? Aaahhh!" I screamed.

I'm in freak out mode now, and I continued to shake my leg. *Oh yeah, my spear!* I reached for my spear, which changed as soon as I touched it.

"What the—" I said but the urgency of the problem was more important than finishing my thought.

The spear turned into a sword. Cool! I attempted to reach the blade between my legs to flick the snakelike vermin off of me, but it squeezed my leg. The numbness felt in my face earlier was now being felt in my leg.

Think Joshua, hurry! Laying on my back I struggled to fight, kick, and fling the creature off of my leg. Getting higher, it was now around my waist.

"Selia, help me!" I screamed, but no such rescue ensued.

I grasped the handle of my sword, closed my eyes and then my sword turned into a clasping claw. *What the heck?* I grasped it off and although its grip had tightened, the claw seemed to work as a weapon for this creature. I threw it and stammered for Selia,

"*Selia...,*" I pleaded.

She still wasn't anywhere I could see. I stood once again and the vermin, which appeared to be a cross between a snake and worm, made its way toward me again. *Are you kidding me? Okay buddy, I got something for you!* This time I was ready, I grabbed it with the claw around its middle, closed my eyes, launched it in the air and my ice spear became an ice sword. *I'm loving this spear!*

Whilst they both fell to the ground, I grabbed the sword, spun and aimed directly at the center, cutting the creature in two. I stood back a bit, not knowing if it could morph into something else or come alive again. Approaching it, I kicked it back into the water hole. No sooner had I done this, the hole closed up, almost as if the whole thing were a figment of my imagination. *Had it been? No, I don't think so.* I looked at my leg, there were small tears where the vermin latched itself on and wouldn't release.

I turned around, Selia was sitting in the snow, seemingly a little dazed.

"Selia, where were you? I needed you and I thought you came along to help. Did you see that thing? It attacked me and if it weren't for my quick thinking skills and weapons, I could have been cut in two!"

"You look fine to me," she smirked.

"Oh my gosh, Selia, you must be here for me. Otherwise, what's the point?" I questioned.

"I'm sorry, Josh. I was observing the other side of this path. I think we can rest up. There's a path between the two mountains. Since it's almost dark, we should rest for the night," she said as if she was not worried about my safety.

"Selia, we seriously need to work on *you* being more alert for both of our sakes," I said, stating the obvious. She just kept walking up the path. I followed.

Alert was my state, I used all senses. I smelled the pine from the leaves of the trees immediately around us, although they were covered with snow, the smell was pungent, a word I learned from my mom. She always said I was pungent with smelly sweat, after I played outside.

Winds always heightened my senses and made my hair stand up. I felt the coolness of it against my face still as I walked. But my eyes, my eyes showed me beautiful things and hidden things too. Fluffy feathered birds feeding their young in nests behind all the leaves on the snow covered trees. Wild animals, I presumed as they were in the wild, hidden in caves, hunkered down with their young.

We stopped before a large rock that overhung a cut-out section of the northern mountain and lay to the left of the southern mountain, just in the center of the valley, which I noticed, when I looked at the map. This was a perfect place to settle for the night.

"Josh, I need your spears," Selia asked.

"My spears? For what? They only work for me, right?" I gave her a quizzical look.

"Yes and no," she answered.

Selia took the spears I handed to her, shook them, and threw them in the air, and out popped a tent and blanketed cots.

"Would you care to rest for the night? We can eat our Power Disk meals and rest up. We'll need it for our long journey tomorrow," she emphatically stated.

"Selia, how did you do that? Back when I was attacked, you could have helped me! Why are you on this journey with me? Ugh!" I asked, not really expecting a satisfactory answer.

Still in shock that my spears could do that, I responded to her silence by entering the tent, sitting down and getting ready for dinner.

The rest of the evening was uneventful. My dinner consisted of an A & W Bacon Cheeseburger, fries, and dessert was my mother's yogurt parfaits she makes with cooked berries. Yum, so delicious! Selia seemed to have eaten her dinner and was fast asleep. I had a difficult time falling asleep, which was always the case when visiting a strange or foreign place. When I'm home, I generally listen to Enya on my computer or with my mom's iPad. No such luck here. We didn't have any electricity. I thought I might be up all night and the sandman wouldn't visit me. Sad news.

I laid down, stared up at the roof of the tent and revisited the day's events; thinking about my family, Gonthragon, Wormly, Pergita, Soran and wondered if I was ever going to set things right here and return home to Hayward. Although, I really didn't have much to return to there, other than my family. After all, a new school awaited me and I probably won't make friends there. *Nobody liked me or thought I was capable of doing great things.* If I could only get my mother and father back together, that would serve my family well. I would be so happy. My mom was really mad at my dad, and my dad will be getting remarried. I continued to think, and I fell asleep.

CHAPTER 14

Dreams are strange. Sometimes they can seem so real and other times they are relaxing and fun. This night, I wasn't quite sure I was dreaming or if I experienced the events, but it felt real.

I walked up a hillside that led to a mountain top and couldn't shake that old sensation of being watched, that same one felt back with the Norkels and in Gonthragon's throne. It made my hair stand up all over my body. Just then a huge squawking gargoyle, which looked familiar, began to fly in my direction. I ran, dodged and darted in and out of trees. My foot slipped and I fell, tumbled head over foot in the snow and off of the side of the mountain.

I reached out and grabbed the gargoyle, which I got the sense was a Thragon. It changed direction to follow me down the side of the mountain. My heart pounded and I tried to grab a rock and my hand slipped. I fell and continued to fall. It was a long drop and barely missed being caught by the Thragon. *Whew, that was close.* Again, I turned head over foot in the snow and rolled downward and picked up speed. I became a large rolling snowball and continued rolling down the side of the mountain. I wiggled my fingers through the side, trying to see, but my vision was blurred by the continuous rolling motion. *Uh oh, I'm feeling a bit nauseated and really need to stop and get off this ride.* To my surprise, I came to an abrupt halt and hit a tree stump. *Ouch! Ohhh, I'm so dizzy. I cannot get up, not now.* I knew the Thargon would soon find me. I had to react quickly. I reached out and grabbed a tree branch that just so happened to be nearby. I placed it over me and dug my feet and hands into the snow. *Please go away, please don't see me.* I heard him overhead and he seemed to be getting closer and closer. Then, nothing, I heard nothing, I saw nothing. I decided to wait a few minutes before I came out of my hiding place. Brrr, I couldn't feel my hands any more. I needed shelter.

Time passed. I shook my head side to side to move the branch slightly to peek out. *Maybe it gave up and went to look somewhere further down the path? I hope so.*

I rubbed my feet together, raised them out of the snow and placed my hands between my legs for warmth. Thawed, I stood up and noticed up above my head there was a clearing where I could build a fire. I ran and hurried toward the open space. Once there, I built a small camouflaged shelter out of branches and leaves. Hoped to fool Thragon or any trespassers with my hideout and needed to warm my body before I moved again. I opened my satchel and took out the fire-starter. *One flick and instant fire. Sweet!* I wiggled my fingers, toes, and whole body in the fire. It defrosted my body quickly.

My mind wandered to the time I met Gonthragon in his chamber, up on his throne and I remembered the vision in the orb. I hated that feeling! A feeling of true outrage and helplessness. I knew I was the one to save these regions, the Norkels, and my family.

Instantly, a claw reached through the leaves and grabbed my arm. I felt myself being pulled downhill. *Ahhh, not again!* Falling, falling, I heard the squawk of the Thragon. He had me in his grasp. I didn't want him to feel victorious because he had me in his grasp. *I have felt victorious, chopping up the snakelike creature on my leg. Wait, was that a dream? Is this a dream?* It didn't feel like a dream and I fell faster and faster. I reached for my satchel, *oh no! My satchel is back near the fire. I have no spears, no weapons, nothing...Oh no, I must do something.* "Help me Selia, help me!" I screamed and kicked with all my might and reached trying to scratch the Thragon's claw. His grasp became tighter and tighter. I saw fire in the distance as I felt my body getting hotter and hotter. Oh, no I'm slipping. *Wait, that's good!* Just then I felt my arm and leg release from the clasp of the Thragon. My body began to fall...and fall and then...suddenly, I woke up!

"Oh, Selia, what happened?" I asked in a sweat.

"You were calling my name, screaming for me, you woke me up!" she exclaimed, gritting her teeth at me.

"Oh no, I'm so sorry, but Selia, I had a bad nightmare I think, but I am not quite sure it was a nightmare, it felt so real. Did we move anywhere? Have we been here the whole time?" I inquired.

"Yes, and it was really hard for me to sleep, you were talking the whole time," she complained.

So I must have been dreaming, but was this just a dream? Are the Thragons out there following us? I was quite sure they were there somewhere, but this dream seemed really real. I wondered if there was another way for us to get up the mountain besides walking up the side. I didn't feel like becoming a falling snowball again.

"Selia, we need to find another way to get to the top of the mountain. I feel as though the snake-like creature and my dream are meant to keep us off the mountain. Do you know of any other way?" I asked her.

"Check your map. We can only follow what's on there," she replied.

She was right. I completely forgot about my map in the mode of panic. Okay, where was it? Let me see. I didn't see my map in my satchel.

"Selia, did you take my map out of my satchel?" I questioned.

"No," she responded. "Do you want me to look outside?"

I nodded my head up and down and she disappeared. *Where could my map be? Was that a dream? Wow, it felt real.* Moments later Selia reappeared, map in hand.

"I found it down the hill near a tree stump. Did you go outside?" she asked as I realized I got my answer to my earlier question. *My dream was real!*

"Selia, we need to be cautious, you said so yourself. The map shows there is an alternative route, but it seems like it's longer," I advised her.

"Well, if you went outside and don't remember and you are feeling unsafe, I think it's wise to take a longer, yet safer route," she said sounding concerned.

We both decided the map was directing us to a safer route. We proceeded through tunnels lined with crystals of some kind that were shiny and glittered as we walked, sort of lighting our path. We traversed bridges made of rope and wood. One of them was dangerous and I nearly fell into the river at the bottom. My spear turned into a mini copter and saved me. Good thing too, I would have died. Rivers that had some slushy water flowing through, instead of completely being frozen over, lined one of our paths.

"Selia, I'm presuming that the map will reveal the Ancient Sacred Tree to me, is that right?" I asked her as we walk and passed by several kinds of trees.

"Yes, I'm sure it will. Have you been looking at it for clues?" Selia seemed curious.

"Hhhmmm, I'm viewing it, but not constantly, I have to pay attention where I walk too," I replied.

I hoped I wasn't missing anything, so I decided to continually monitor the map.

We continued to walk along the path revealed on the map and it seemed accurate, which I believe wasn't the case when we decided to travel through the valley. Perhaps we'll have a safer time this way.

As daylight came to an end, we both decided it was time to stop. We found a decent place to stop and this time Selia placed a spell on the tent, which prevented me from escaping and intruders from getting in.

"Why didn't you use that last night?" I asked her.

"Unfortunately, I cannot use a spell unless it's required. My magic and specialties are very limited. It's to prevent abuse of my powers," she replied.

"Selia, who has the power to limit your powers?" I asked.

"Joshua, you are the chosen one. It's in the prophecy. I cannot make decisions. I only respond to the needs arising out of your encounters, decisions, and such." Selia stated making a new revelation.

"Well, I'm glad you're along the journey with me. Thanks for being my friend, I don't—" I was cut off.

"—have many, I know," she said, smiling at me.

We slept. This time the night was uneventful. *Thank goodness!*

CHAPTER

I opened my eyes and stared up once again at the roof to our tent. Selia's spell really worked, I didn't remember dreaming last night and nothing penetrated the boundaries of our tent. Relief was felt throughout my body. Selia sat on the edge of her cot, in some strange yoga position. Her eyes were closed and she chanted something. *Strange. I needed to pack.*

I gathered my belongings and made sure everything was tucked nicely inside of my satchel. Grateful to Wormly for giving it to me, it was no ordinary bag. Upon further inspection and after using it, I discovered it allowed me pack it full of anything, however, the weight remained the same. Long journeys were much easier with a "lightweight" satchel.

After I packed, I checked the map for any changes or messages which could alter our course. I noticed an addition, the path seemed to be diverting toward a body of water.

"Hey Selia, it looks like our path is about the get a little wet. There's a body of water added to the end of our path," I said as I directed her attention to the map.

"Well, are you hungry?" she asked.

We took a moment to eat our Power Disks, nourishing ourselves before our journey. Mine was a ham and egg sandwich with milk. I was in heaven. I loved ham.

We started following the map, which led us in the opposite direction we were traveling yesterday, but not yet back to our original starting point. The snow was pure and glistened in the sun. As we walked, it blinded us by its brightness. Snow covered mountains, branches, rocks, caves and it if weren't for the map, I wouldn't believe water surrounded us anywhere.

Selia was behind me as we trekked through the snow. I felt uneasy about her constant separation from me. Unfortunately, each time she did, weird things happened.

We seemed to be walking for about an hour, time passed quickly. Distant noises stopped me in my tracks. Faint as it was, I couldn't quite make it out and uncertain if it was the wind howling or a voice talking, but the familiarity of it soothed me.

"Goooo bbbaaak" was the sound I heard, but it was unclear. I strained my ears, moved my hood nearest my left ear to listen to the traveling sound waves and decipher the sound. I heard it about four times, then I stopped, but when I did the sound disappeared.

"Dang it, what was that? I wish it would sound again. Selia, did you hear that?" I questioned as I turned around.

She wasn't behind me. In the distance, a dark shadowy thing moved toward me. Although I couldn't see Selia, my immediate concern was the shape that gained ground on me. *My hiking boots. They are equipped with snowshoe nets and ski-style skates.* I pushed a switch on the back of my boots! *Whoah! I hit warp speed.*

Skiing caused the snow to fly in the wind as I snow skated further from the sound. I thought I caught a glimpse of a shape, but was not sure. The sky started to blacken, although it was only late morning, I felt a storm coming on. My breath quickened as I moved around trees, hills, rocks and hoped Selia was wise enough to follow me. The wind kicked it up a notch and was so strong that it began to impact my forward motion. *Oh, I can't keep this up, it's exhausting. I must stop.* I turned around, no sight of Selia or anything that might have followed me. I ducked down inside an opening between two rocks and a tree. Rapidly breathing now, I needed to catch my breath, while also not being heard. I focused on my breathing and used strategies to slow it down. Yoga classes at school really helped me at this point. My eyes were closed and my heartbeat slowed to a rhythmic pattern of someone at rest. Selia's yoga pose immediately came to mind.

I opened my eyes and tried to adjust them, it seemed to be some kind of cave. Just then, I noticed them, two yellowish brown eyes stared in my direction and then it growled. It sounded like a deeper version of my pet, Sara, when she growled at the mailman. My heart froze and not because of the snow! Horrified, I slowly backed up toward the entrance, so slow as to give the impression I wasn't moving. Just as I thought my trickery was my magic at work, the growl increased in volume and I had to turn and run. My mind raced to think of the equipment in my satchel. *Okay, I have an ice spear, spears, fire, melt snow/water, walking tennis rackets, rope, is that all I have? No...wait, oh yes the crystal whip. I still have that from when I tamed the goose or whatever that thing was and it will hopefully work on this thing.* As I ran, I tried to open my satchel and rummage around in it with my hand, all while trying to keep away from the wild beast that had begun to run toward me. *Come on, where is it? I feel the rope, which might come in handy later.* I can't seem to find it, *wait a minute. Oh yes, here it is,* as I pulled it out, I started to slow down and turned around, smack! I ran into the branch of a tree covered in snow, so much that I couldn't see the tree. I tumbled over and lost the grip on the whip. *Oh my, where is it?* I quickly scanned the area, hoping to tame the beast. As I looked up I stared at snarling teeth, yellowish eyes that seemed to be searching for my inner soul as it kept me pinned on the ground. My heart was beating out of my chest and I felt like I was going to pee my pants. I also remembered my spear could transform. Frightened, but full of daring heroic qualities I reached inside my satchel and the beast lunged at my arm, grabbed hold of my jacket and began penetrating my jacket. I felt the searing of my flesh within the jacket, as his teeth dug deeper. I had my fingertips on my spear, but I couldn't quite grasp it. My neck was clenched in its jaws. I saw my life flash before my eyes and thoughts of my mother, father, and my siblings brought me to tears. I wasn't going to give up! —I stretched further, captured the spear, swung it out and just then the crystal whip fell out of its mouth. I quickly grabbed it, tied it around its neck and it stopped biting. My heart was still beating about one hundred thousand miles per hour, and I sweated profusely. My arm throbbed and just then Selia showed up.

"WHERE HAVE YOU BEEN?" I inquired, looking beat up.

"I'm sorry, I'm not able to help you in battles, just so you know," she said with her head down.

"Okay, well then you're no good to me are you? I mean I almost died and I just knew I was done for. That thing, that creature, beast thing ...well, it attacked me after a very long chase," was my response.

"So that first chase wasn't the beast, it was me. I was trying to catch up to you and I knew that the further behind you I got, the less likely you were to see me. So I picked up speed and ran. Sorry I startled you," she remarked as she began to pet the now tame beast.

"What! You? Okay, we're not friends anymore Selia, you freaked me out!" I said glaring at her.

"You were on those skis or skates, whatever they are and I couldn't catch you," she said apologetically.

"Okay, but why aren't you around when I get attacked? Huh?" I asked.

"I told you, I can't help, but you did fine in the end, right? You're alive. You're here!" she said.

I walked over to her. She was petting the now tame creature.

"You know what? This looks like a wolf to me, Selia. We have them in specific places in my home and some people think they are vicious. Well, in this case I would agree, but they actually can be quite tame," I advised as I examined the animal and spoke to her.

Snow began to fall harder and I mentioned the cave I found earlier, before the chase.

"You mean about five miles ago," Selia quietly mentioned.

"Really, that far? Well, I'm a bit tired and could use some first aid. I'm bleeding and now the snow isn't so white," I showed her as I kick at the ground.

"We need nourishment from our Power Disk after that we can get you first aid. We just have to do it quickly, we need to keep moving, we should cover more ground before it gets dark," she said as she motioned up the hill to the north.

We stopped, Selia made a tent as before, we ate and Selia materialized with a first aid kit, which to her was only because it was needed and hence the reason she could provide it. I recalled what she told me the other day about her helping when the time called for it. I guess any help, no matter how small can be a big help.

She continued to wipe my wounds and as it turned out, I needed stitches. She placed her hand on my upper arm and closed her eyes. I felt as if all feeling left my arm and she hurriedly stitched me up with a needle and thread which appeared instantly. I needed about five stitches. We gathered our things and set off on our journey again.

"We ought to take it slowly and this beast can be our protection from other creatures, or at least a deterrent to attacks, until we reach our destination," Selia calmly spoke as we got under way.

By now the snow had stopped and the sun was beginning to come out again. I picked up the map and examined it. We were very close to the watery area on the map, so close we looked off in the distance and could see the edges of it. Bluish green waves were splashing up against the beach area and trees lined the shores. We walked, the beast alongside of us, like an Akiak would if it were headed off to the Iditarod, pumped out chest and without a sled.

We approached the water in about twenty minutes, as the sun continued to beat down on us.

"Selia, it's hot. Can you hold my jacket so I can check where the map shows we should go?" I said as I removed my jacket and handed it to her.

"Sure, I can do that." replied Selia.

"And the beast? I need both hands," I said, passing command of the whip to Selia.

She could handle the beast so I could view the map and determine the next phase on our journey.

Examination of the map revealed we were to head through the water and stop on the other side about ten nautical miles around the bend, which was where more mountains seem to be. *Hhhmmm, this journey isn't very easy. I guess whoever hid the Ancient Sacred Tree really didn't want it to be found by accident.*

"Selia?" I called to her, but got no answer.

"Selia?" Again no answer.

So I looked up. I saw Selia staring directly at me, but empty handed. She stood at the edge of the water, but the beast was gone.

"What happened?" I asked her, my eyes widened, but on purpose this time, not because they were working magically.

"Uh, I came to the edge of the water because the beast was pulling me in that direction, then, its paws touched the water and..." She stopped talking.

"Yes, and...and what?" I inquired of her.

"Well...it, uh...it changed," she muttered.

"Selia, what are you talking about and why would it change? Is the whip around its neck?" I questioned her.

"The beast changed. It changed into a winged whale creature. It dove into the water. Look over there," she said.

I looked off into the distance and sure enough, I could see the creature she described jumping in and out of the water, the whip was still attached to its neck or I would have thought the beast drowned or escaped. I couldn't believe my eyes. What kind of thing was this that could change its shape? My question made me remember all the Wolverine movies I'd watched and some Star Trek episodes with shapeshifters. I was really intrigued by the sight of it all.

The creature came over to the edge of the water and seemed to want us to approach it. Selia and I moved in and as soon as I felt water on my boot. A slimy, yet hard-skinned thing pushed me closer to the water and onto the back of our new mode of transportation.

"Whoa," we both said in unison looking at each other.

"Well, I guess we know how we are supposed to get to the next part of the map," I told Selia as she just looked at me.

I never would have guessed it, a beast "land to water" creature. Although it tried to kill me, I grew quite fond of our new life-saving friend.

We cruised across the water smoothly traversing waves. The air was fresh and smelled of sea salt, similar to the oceans back home in my world. We noticed no other animals in the water and dangled our feet on the side of the creature. It was refreshing and surprisingly warm compared to the frozen snow.

"Selia, I think I'm going to call our new friend Akhlut, which is some type of mythical orca-wolf creature," I told her, remembering stories my mother told me when I was young.

Selia just shrugged and held on tight to my jacket and satchel.

Akhlut was not hairy. His skin was smooth like a whale, but deep purple in color. The wings were similar to a fish's fins, no feathers or fur, just smooth like the rest of its body. The Akhlut's tail was wispy and a lavender blue. It stroked our heads with it as we sailed along on our journey. Lastly, my favorite part, its lashes. The Akhlut's eyes were yellow with a purple pupil and lavender lashes, the color of its wispy tail. The noise it made was like a dolphin when we glided across the water. I knew he was talking to us.

Time passed quickly. It wasn't before long that we saw land just ahead and prepared for dismounting Akhlut as I reviewed the map once again.

CHAPTER

ismounting meant getting a bit wet, but we weren't really concerned since both of us were drenched from the ride. Selia suggested a fire to dry out our clothes, which sounded good to me and provided more time to examine the map.

We said goodbye to our friend, hoping we'd see Ahkhut again, but I doubted it. I placed my whip back into my satchel and admired the surroundings. The air was crisp with a bit of warmth sprinkled by the sun shining brightly. The sky was bluish purple, reflective of the water below it and the clouds eerily were not in suit with the sky. They were dark gray. Weird sight if you asked me. As I gazed around, I tried to find a place for us to rest.

Selia dried our clothes whilst I glanced down at the map. I noticed the trees were losing their leaves, which caused the snow to fall revealing more of the tree itself. I took note of it as this could become important as we continued our journey.

"Selia, over here, this place looks as good as any and I'm eager to get us moving along our journey to a more secluded place," I said as she followed me.

Selia was helpful, but I missed my mom's magic touch to make me feel better. I reminisced about her. Although Selia provided excellent medical attention, my mom had a warmth about her and a tender approach, which I guess most moms do. I wished she were here with us now and thinking of her I began to daydream. While I daydreamed, I saw this vision on my map:

Flying above into the sky gave me a bird's-eye view of the whole city. I spot my mother driving in her gold Geo Prizm up Highway 101. She actually had my Seneca journal on the seat next to her. I heard someone say that curiosity killed the cat, which seemed to get the better of me as I examined the memory banks of my brain to figure out why she had it and where she was going. I didn't recognize the highway she was on. We'd never taken it before. I flew a little closer to her car window. I flew right alongside when the phone rang and my mother answered.

"I'm on the highway. Did you find Jake's journal?" my mother questioned the caller.

I couldn't hear the response given, but the only person I could imagine they knew where my dad's journal was, just happened to live up north. We were in their house for maybe five minutes before vanishing to Gonthragon's chamber.

She hung up the phone and seemed to be irritated. She increased her speed. Mario Andrade had nothing on my mother. She could drive faster than most racecar drivers and the next thing I knew, I had to fly higher to avoid getting squished, as she exited the freeway.

The road was secluded. The location seemed to be uninhabited as my mom's car drove along a narrow roadway. Redwood trees and various ferns lined the highway and intermittent sunshine weaved in and out of trees where shadows formed between them. Green moss lined a small wooden fence about three feet high to the left of the road. Birds chirped in the distance and I noticed a flight of butterflies, monarchs I believed, also lined the fence. I recalled my mother taking us somewhere similar to this place and butterflies would land all over us. Perhaps this was the place we visited, but I couldn't be sure. As she drove along this road, I began to think about contacting her. Did my mom feel my presence? She had to know I was safe and that I've seen dad and Leilani. Thinking quickly, I wondered if I could write something with my—*oh dang it, I'm not really there, and I don't have my spear, or do I? As luck would have it, magical things happen in dreams.* I grabbed my spear and flew closer to the car. The window was slightly opened, so I craftily wedged my spear inside and gently pushed open the journal, which made a sound like pages swishing and caught my mother's attention. She rolled up the window, dang near taking off my hand. *I hate it when she does that, she's always doing that back home.* Okay, this was going to be harder than I thought. Perhaps the Ice Plant Ink will help me out. I carefully opened the area in the handle and began to dip the spear inside. Now, if only I could mentally air-write a message and just as I thought, I saw words take shape on the book inside my mom's car.

"*YES!*"

"Mom, it's me Josh, I'm okay. I saw Leilani and dad. I need you to meet at the Tree near dad's house," …*what, where did that come from? How do I know that? I feel a battle within my head, but continued to write.*

Message will come through the leaves. You'll hear or see. Stay safe and nearby.

Love,

Josh

My ink was out, but the message seemed complete, although I didn't quite know where the information about the tree came from...so strange.

I woke up, saw Selia sitting up, but not looking at me. She was trancelike and as soon as I noticed this, her eyes opened.

"Your mother got your message. She's going to camp out near the tree at your dad's new house, after she gets the journal from your dad's new wife. Let's hope there's only one tree there," Selia advised me.

"What?" I said, "How do you know?"

"I'm here to help," she said.

"Selia, I did not imagine or think to inform my mother about a tree. What's going on? Was that you that popped that idea into my thoughts?" I asked intrigued. "Oh, and they aren't quite married, not yet!" I replied angrily.

"Yes," she said, "I'm here to help you, remember?"

CHAPTER

Jake was new to this journey and adventure type of life. He was not really into getting his hands dirty, but his son's well-being was at stake and he knew he must pull through. Not knowing where to start except for the hospital that fixed Joshua many years ago he headed off to find a way to get back to reality.

Well, I know that my son's wishfulness to see me, and the need to get his spear forced me into some kind of portal with him. However, I'm not quite sure I have the tools for that. Dang, Josh, you could have left your old man with some kind of weapon, you know I'm no James T. Kirk. I can't just get beamed up. "Hhhmmm, well what if I imagine or dream of home, maybe *that will help. Heaven knows I don't have any tools, spells, or special magical powers.*

As soon as Jake said that, he was lifted off the ground and shot like a rocket through what seemed to be a tube or tunnel…

"Whoa, ouch, ooh, ewe, uh…kablam…," were sounds emanating from within Jake's mouth, just as he landed on the floor of the Eden Hospital in Castro Valley, California.

What in the world? H-h-how? Oh, never mind. I had to get to the medical records department, I wonder what time it is? Jake questioned himself while picking himself off the floor and peering around corners, looking for a directory or map.

Jake wandered the halls, searched inside rooms. He found a doctor's white coat inside of one, removed the name and slipped it on as he continued on his quest.

The walls were freshly painted white with fire extinguishers, oxygen tanks, and wheelchairs placed on or up against them throughout the hall he was currently in with no sign of a map or directory. As he crossed the next hall, he noticed a nurse's information section. He approached.

"Hello, can you please direct me to the records department?" Jake asked in desperation.

"What is it you need? We have many records in this hospital, sir. May I be of assistance to you? Who is it you're looking for?" asked the nurse behind the counter who appeared to be a volunteer in a red and white nurse's uniform.

"Well, the person I'm looking for stayed in the hospital about four to six years ago. Do you keep records that far in the past?" he questioned her.

"Oh, I'm sorry, but that department is currently being renovated and they are currently being stored in the temporary records department, which is located at this address," she replied apologetically, as she wrote down an address and handed it to him.

Jake read the address as he thanked her and searched for the elevator. The address appeared to be one a few miles away, so he would have to take the bus, his car was in Eureka.

The street was lined with cars parked on either side of it and just outside the hospital on Lake Chabot Road there was a bus stop. Luckily he kept his wallet which had a few dollars inside, just enough to pay for the bus and get a burger for lunch.

As he waited for the bus, he noticed the sky was baby blue with wispy cirrus clouds dispersed evenly as far as he could see. The streets were not really busy for this time of day. He glanced at his watch. He confirmed the time to be 3:18 p.m., which meant the records department should still be open.

He hadn't been waiting too long when he spotted the green, orange, and silver bus approaching. He made sure the bus was number 22, boarded, and paid the $1.25. He sat down in the fourth row next to a young boy carrying a backpack. He smiled and proceeded to stare out of the window. The young lad was busy playing some game on his iPhone and ignored Jake.

San Leandro Boulevard was his destination. He knew he had about a thirty-minute trip ahead of him.

Staring out of the window, Jake began to see familiar landmarks from when he lived in San Leandro and Hayward. They just passed Connie's Tropical Fish, and he remembered when he took the kids to buy fish for their fish tank and crickets for their pet turtle. Daydreaming about those days made the time travel fast because when Jake looked up he was already on San Leandro Boulevard. He prepared to depart the bus.

Jake looked at his watch, it was 3:50. The medical records department must still be open, he thought.

Jake walked around the corner and noticed several medical buildings, so he pulled out the paper with the address on it. The building with the matching address was directly in front of him. He inspected the outside of the building, a green and white painted little house with a sign SRC Building painted on it. Wondering what that meant, he walked up the pathway made from river rock and small pebbles. Several green shrubs lined the outside walls of the small office complex and the double door also had planted tall trees, perhaps cacti of some kind, lining the sides of the entryway.

Jake knocked on the door and then noticed the sign that read:

Please come in. Door is open.

Inside, he found a plain office, white walls, white desks and counter space. The two clerks inside were busy entering information into the computers.

"I'll be right with you, sir," said the lady closest to the counter.

Jake sat in a chair in the empty waiting room. He was the only person waiting and hoped he wouldn't be waiting long.

"Sir, I can help you now," said the same voice he heard when he entered.

"Hi, I'm interested in getting information about a donor that supplied my son with an eye about six years ago," Jake asked.

"Okay sir, I'll need you to complete this form and I'll need your driver's license for identification purposes," she informed him.

Taking the form and handing her his license, Jake began to look over the papers. He started filling out as much information as he could remember and then thought about calling Noel, Joshua's mom. She would have more information since she filled out his medical forms and kept all those types of records. Jake asked to use the phone, but had no luck reaching Noel by phone.

Hoping he had enough information, he took the form back to the clerk.

"This is all I can remember, I'm not able to get in touch with my ex-wife. She's the one with all the information," Jake told the clerk.

"It's okay, I'll try with what you've provided, here's your License, please have a seat," she responded.

Jake sat and began to read an article in the Times about NFL players to pass the time. He looked up at the clock and it was almost 5:00 p.m. He walked up to the counter, just as the clerk stood up.

"Okay, sir, I've found very little information, but the person you are looking for is actually in another hospital. You are listed in one section of the file, so I can reveal the address to you. You can find the person you're searching for at the Masonic Homes in Union City," the clerks said as she wrote the address on Mission down. "Visiting hours are until 8:00 p.m., so if you hurry, you can make those today," she said with a smile.

Jake took the address and was very curious now. He remembered passing that place several times while living in Hayward. The kids used to think it was creepy and haunted. He felt a sense of eeriness inside as he recollected those occasions in his mind. He knew he had to get there tonight, but he didn't have a car and he used the last bit of change he had on the bus fare, which only allowed him to get one transfer. He would transfer back to Foothill and walk the rest of the way.

Jake took the twenty-two back toward the hospital, but got off in Hayward on Foothill. He continued to walk for almost two hours, the time it took him to walk down Foothill to Mission and through Hayward to Union City.

Jake observed the scenery as he made his way up the hill. The hills were lined and covered by mostly dried grasslands and every now and again, green grass spots were noticed. Either side of the home stood vacant fields, also full of grass. Political signs from the latest election were lining the fence that surrounded the home. Way up the hillside, there was a worn dirt path where hikers and Regional Parks' workers hiked or drove for years. The actual path he walked on was lined with eucalyptus trees and seemed to "hide" the homes from street viewers.

Climbing up the hill on the pathway to the Masonic Homes, he tried to figure out what he would say to this strange man. He only met him once in the hospital.

Jake made it to the front door and entered. The lady at the records department he just left had given him a copy of the paper with the old man's name on it. She advised him it would be beneficial in gaining access to see the old man.

Jake approached the counter and handed the paper to the lady behind the counter.

"Please wait here, sir," and she left.

"Okay, thank you," Jake responded.

Thirty minutes later the lady came back and said, "I'm sorry sir, this man isn't here any longer. He died."

"What? But—" was all he could get out of his mouth before someone touched him on his shoulder.

Jake turned around and without conversation was led by a security guard to a meeting room and told to wait. After a few minutes the door opened and in walked a man with grayish white wiry hair, a long beard and one-eyed glasses. He hunched over a walker as he moved and sat in a rocker to the left of Jake. His skin was as dark as Jake's but wrinkled and looked a bit worn. His head was tilted down as he peered at his feet, but then his head turned and looked at Jake.

"Hello, what is it you are searching for," inquired the old man.

"Uh sir, I'm in need of some answers. My son," Jake began, but was cut off by the old man.

"I know your son. We met several years ago in the hospital. He has my other eye and now you seek help. He's in need of information about me and the eye, his abilities are endless you know?" the old man spoke with great awareness and conviction.

"Yes, I need to know why you chose my son and what type of magical powers are inside of the eye you gave him? He's currently lost in a magical world and he's supposed to save everyone! He's eight and not sure why he's been chosen.

I'm also not quite sure, but it was recommended I travel to see you," Jake told the old man.

Just then Jake noticed tears flowing from the old man's eyes, which began when he started to speak, but were flowing more abundantly now.

"Please, take these tears. They are necessary ingredients to help Joshua fight and defeat the evil side of any enemy posing harm to him. You can also find hidden secrets in the journal that Joshua is seeking, hidden by your fiancé. Noel is there now trying to recoup it. She will not succeed as it's been foretold you or Joshua are the only two that can possibly grapple with her and the journal she has is fake," the old man revealed to Jake.

Jake stared at the old man and spoke, "What secrets are hidden inside that journal? I wrote its contents, how can there be secrets unknown to me?" Jake questioned him, but he wouldn't get any answers, the old man suddenly disappeared into thin air. Jake stood up and walked to the door. He peered outside, but nobody was around. The staff at the front desk were gone and lights were all out.

Jake headed to the door and the trees began to blow as a wind picked up. He could hear the wind, it seemed to whisper, "be safe, you've been tricked, be warned," as he walked down the pathway. Jake wasn't quite sure what had just transpired and ignored the wind. He must find a way to get back home. He must get his journal and find a way to get the tears to Joshua.

CHAPTER

Mom pulled of the road and searched for the address. She noticed the journal on the seat was opened and read it. Her face looked as if she'd seen a ghost. Her head whipped around as she searched under the seat and peered outside of the window. "Joshua?" she called.

She got out of the car. Frantically, she ran around the car, peering underneath and called out for him once more. She put her head in her hands, she shook it, and then stared toward the sky.

"Joshua!" she screamed.

Joshua did not emerge and she got back into the car, picked up the journal, and reread what was written.

Noel was puzzled, but the message seemed to calm her a bit. Instantly, she found the paper with the address on the floor of the car, she looked at it. There was a house just off the side of the road, perhaps she had made it to the house. Exiting the car, she grabbed Josh's journal and tucked it underneath her arm.

Walking up the cobblestone path, she noticed a brick house with ivy climbing the walls and gargoyle figurines along the walkway. Nervously she double checked the address. "Yes, this is it," Noel said aloud and hesitantly walked forward.

Approaching the door she began to feel "watched" and picked up the knocker to announce her arrival. Just as she did, it opened and inside was a woman in a black dress. Her face was a bit worn. She had a long pointed nose and dark brown eyes. *Hhmm, she's shorter than I thought.*

"Come in, you must be Noel," said the woman, she called herself Kate.

"Hello Kate, thank you," responded Noel "I'm glad I made it safely, such a winding road and you seem to be tucked in away from the road," she attempted to make conversation.

"Yes, we like our privacy. So after our phone conversation I went searching for the journal Jake keeps and couldn't' find it anywhere.

"Oh?" Noel said.

"We went to church last Sunday and I'm sure it's there. I have phoned the pastor and he says quite a number of people leave things behind. He's waiting for you if you'd like to make your way there now," Kate said.

Noel remembered the note in the journal tucked under her arm. She was supposed to wait by a tree near this house, so she decided this must be kept secret, but she noticed the look on Kate's face was seeming to search her own face for answers.

"Oh, that's just fine, I guess I'll be on my way then. I don't want to trouble you too much, but I'm in your debt. Thank you," Noel said to Kate as she exited the door with yet a new destination.

I wonder which tree is "the tree" Joshua is referring to. Noel meandered off the path of the one leading to the house to find something unusual about any trees around the area. Just then a bird or something flew by her arm and knocked the journal. The journal fell open to the page Joshua wrote on, and immediately wind began to gust up, leaves flew around, and it appeared the leaves were making their way toward a tall pine tree in the distance. Noel leaned over, picked up the journal, and followed the leaves. She began to run to keep pace with the leaves as they suddenly moved faster. Then, just as suddenly as the wind appeared, it stopped. The leaves fell and there directly in front of Noel was a tree, standing a good four hundred feet tall. She felt a sense of calm and knew this must be the tree Joshua mentioned in the journal.

She made her way back to the car and searched her map for directions to the church. She planned to get the journal and then travel back to the tree. She did not know when the message was due to come forth so she hurried.

I decided to peer through my spear again. This time I caught a glimpse of my mother near the tree and knew she found it. *Great job, Mom!*

Noel approached the address of the church and exited her car. Gargoyles seemed to be everywhere. She noticed them on the building of the church. Leery of this fact, Noel decided to put Joshua's journal under her arms for protection. Dark greenish painted crosses encircled the gargoyles. She found several gargoyles were at the end of the pathway, but the door was opened. Entering the church, it appeared empty. She walked around and saw books stacked, jackets boxed, and robes that hung in the closet. Walking over to them she noticed a flyer on the wall, Lost and Found, and decided this must be where she'd find the journal. She began to look through the stacked books.

She placed the first book onto the table and created a second stack, but every book in the church started to fly around the room and twisted in every direction. Noel was frightened and began to run. She wasn't quite sure what was going on, but she wasn't about to stick around to find out. She opened the door, since she had closed it and books begin to fly outside of the church, as they followed her. She opened the door and got into her car. The books that chased her smacked into her windows. One even caused her window to crack. She jumped, screamed, and then noticed a huge gargoyle overhead trying to land on the car. She backed out, peeled down the driveway, and left dust and leaves behind her. The gargoyle wasn't deterred as it continued to follow her and tried to place its claws on the top of her car. It clasped hold of the antennae and grabbed the car, making Noel slide all over the road as the right side of the car lifted off the road. Noel slammed on the brakes and the gargoyle lost its grip. Noel detoured off the road back down the road that led to Jake's house and toward the tree. She drove the car directly in front of the tree and stopped. Turning around, she noticed Kate. She stood directly outside of her car door. Noel screamed and then suddenly relaxed. She rolled down the window and Kate began to talk to her in an apologetic tone.

"I don't know what's happening. As soon as I met Jake, I noticed flying creatures all over the church. I'm not sure if he's possessed or not, but I've been wanting to talk to you about this. You see, the journal isn't the only reason I wanted to you to come up here. We need to talk," Kate emphatically said to Noel.

Noel was stunned. She had noticed some strange things about Jake before the divorce. This all seemed to make sense, and she didn't think to question Kate.

"Yes, I've noticed this too. You think it's Jake that caused those gargoyles to chase me?" Noel asked Kate.

Just then she realized, she hadn't mentioned this to Kate and quietly wondered how she knew.

"I found Jake's journal while you were gone, he must have hidden it under his bed, which was where I found it," Kate assured Noel.

Noel and Kate began to talk as Noel opened the door to the car for Kate to sit alongside of her. As they continued to talk I picked up the spear, looked through the end and witnessed their conversation. *Kate was trying to make dad look bad!*

My dad isn't bad, and Mom must know this. I cannot believe she's listening to Kate. I'm angry. I have to send a message to her, but I know Kate will intercept it. What can I do?

Just then my spear stopped working and I knew I must reach Soran for help.

Selia was near me, but then I remembered the map. I began to draw a picture of Soran when all at once, he appeared…inside the map, he motioned me forward. I walked on and into a cloudy area.

"What is it Joshua?" Soran asked.

"My mother is under a spell. She's by the tree. I saw her, but no longer can see her. My ink is gone," I said to him.

"You know Selia can help when there's a need? She can help you deliver a message to your mother. Ask her," Soran told me. "And Joshua, please hurry, our land cannot hold out much longer. Our habitants are becoming Thragons and Gonthragon is burning everything!" Soran sadly reminded me.

"I'm trying," I assured Soran just before I tapped Selia and asked for help. Selia took the spear and then gave it back to me.

"You can send another message, make it a good one," she told me with urgency.

I send a message through the tree and then pine needles begin to write this message on my journal:

Mom, you're under Kate's spell, she's a witch…dad is good, looking for Shaman, get the journal and get out.

CHAPTER

My mother sat in the car with Kate, the witch. I sure hope she got my message. Accomplishing this task required the help of my family. No way could I do it without them. I wished I knew where my dad was and how his journey was going, but I couldn't waste my only means to "see" into my real world to find out. Mom was in real danger and I had to make sure she knew dad wasn't the evil one.

Selia and I were positioned on top of a mountain. We stopped to consume our Power Disks and rejuvenate our bodies. I hoped my last communication efforts with my mom worked. She was my only hope to get back home.

Glances at my map were quite frequent, since Selia and I conversed about its importance. I noticed it began to change color, the whole thing was now a forest of trees, but as suddenly as they appeared, they started to burn. Smoke swirled everywhere across my map. I turned, Selia looked into the distance. Tears flowed down her face and I knew this was all bad. We both began to run toward the trees and Selia fell directly in front of one, bent over and bowed down as if to worship it.

"You found it! We found it! That's the tree, right?" I asked.

The Ancient Sacred Tree burned before our eyes.

"Selia, we have to do something, it's burning down!" I screamed.

"It's too late, we are too late to save it!" she cried.

"Selia, no. There must be something we can do!" I hollered.

"Joshua, we've talked about this. Unless your parents meet each other, we are doomed here and you'll never make it home. We've failed to save the tree. Look at it—it's ashes!" she raised her voice to reply.

I stood there, we stood there, stunned and mouths hung open. I noticed there was still a small area that was on fire. *I got this!*

"Your parents must figure out a plan together and do it out of true love for you," Selia said, as I tried to put out the fire.

Moments later we stood in front of fried trees. The whole area was consumed with smoke, ash, and not a tree was standing, including the one I tried to save. I was stunned and felt defeated. I fell into the snow and began to cry.

"I just cannot believe this has all been for nothing. I failed," I cried.

Selia put her arm around me and tried to comfort me, but it was all for not.

Back home, I felt bad about myself, but not here, until now. *I'm never good at anything, I can't do anything by myself.* Gloom and sadness swallowed me and it seemed all hope was lost.

Thoughts of my mother, my sister, my old school, and my therapist rushed into my mind. I remembered all those times we sat in family therapy and talked about coping skills and tools that I could use to feel better and control my emotions. I recalled the grounding exercises Michelle taught me, especially the metaphors she would use. I felt a sense of warmth and security for these memories, yet defeated as I sat and realized my whole journey was over. My mission had failed.

I'm no hero. *Why did I believe I could do this? Who was I kidding? Myself, that's who and everyone in this alternate world that believed in me.* I would disappoint Wormly, Soran, Pergita, and Selia, most of all Leilani and my mother who were out there fighting. *How could mom get all the way to my dad's house if it weren't for me? Hmm, it must have been dad or someone that convinced her to go, right?*

I opened my satchel and began taking out the contents and tried to find something that we could use to get back. I threw my spear, my rope, my whip, my water, Power Disks, and fire-starters. Oh and my jacket, I hated it and was too upset to be cold.

Selia walked over and picked up the tools I threw out. She stood there, picked up the water starter, turned and said, "You have the power to take us back to a time when the tree wasn't burnt down yet. We can use the water-starter and put it out!"

"No, I'm no hero, it's too late, you said so yourself," I said.

"Josh, I'm serious!" she said and reached for the map and water-starter and handed them both to me!

Wait, she's right! I control the map, well…my mind does, but I can make that happen.

"Genius," I told her. "You are completely genius!"

Ashes covered my map, but I brushed them aside and began to draw Selia and myself climbing up the mountain, just like we had done about an hour or two ago. The tree was intact, just as it was before. At once the creature that turned into a goose approached me at light speed, I dashed his attack and grabbed my whip. I disentangled it just in the nick of time and threw it around the creature's neck. It twisted and flipped back and forth. Within minutes, I saw the beautiful goose that flew me around earlier in my journey.

"Okay Selia, I'm going to jump on and fly toward the tree," I told her.

The goose swooped, I flung myself onto its back and we were headed directly for the tree. *Dang it, the water's in the pile of tools I threw out.*

"Selia, I need my water. I forgot it," I screamed down to her.

"Come back, I'll come with you! You'll need two hands anyway!" she said.

We flew down and picked up Selia.

"Okay I'll dangle down the whip as you release the water. We'll sprinkle and release it, since the end of this whip can turn into a fan," she said.

Selia was so genius and helpful. She immediately dispersed the water throughout the forest as I released it to her. Our last bit of water fell directly over, around and onto the Ancient Sacred Tree! We flew on top of it and released the goose, who immediately began to twist and turn back into the scaly creature.

Selia and I opened my satchel and transferred the tea leaves from the tree to my satchel.

"Thank goodness we saved the tree, it's the last one of its kind," said Selia.

"My satchel can carry as many as we need. It's a weightless bag," I said.

When the tea leaves were mixed with the Ice Plant Ink, it allowed me to see using the spear. I needed this to continue to help mom.

"Good, we'll stock up! Josh, do you know you can not only see into your world or other parts of our world with the spear, ink, and leaves, you can see into entire other worlds?" Selia revealed to me.

"What other worlds, aren't there only two? Yours and mine," I replied.

"No, there are thousands or at least I was told," she said.

"Wow! Now that would be an adventure, but I think I'll stick close to home for a while. Well…when I get home," I responded.

Selia continued to pack the satchel to stock up on the leaves, whilst I placed some onto the spear, which enabled me to see Gonthragon. As I peered into the spear I witnessed the horrifying event that earlier was predicted in my vision. He was burning the land of the Norkels, the Ice Plants were one quarter burned, grasslands entirely burnt, and all trees that surrounded his castle, except the ones on the inside were burned. I watched as homes in Hayward burned. Smoke engulfed the city.

The vision changed. Mom talked to Kate, but I sensed mom knew that dad wasn't bad,

"I must leave now Kate, nice meeting you," mom said.

"Bye Noel," Kate said.

Kate left mom's car and mom picked up the phone. She called dad, since she missed an earlier call from him.

"Jake, how are you? I just left your house and Kate was trying to brainwash me," Noel said to Jake.

"Noel, I know, I have some news for you too and I'm on my way there. I need to get my journal. Do you want to meet at the Shell station in Ukiah?" Jake asked Noel.

"Okay, but Kate has your journal and I think she's intending on doing something horrible," mom said and agreed to meet Jake at the station.

Wait, where's the vision? I looked at my spear. Oh, my Ice Plant Ink is gone, I must get more.

CHAPTER

I needed to talk to Mom and Dad! Since they were going to meet at a gas station in Ukiah, I could make it there too, but how?

Hhmm, Mom had my journal. Maybe I could write another message for her since she was no longer near a tree to hear the leaves. Wait, what? Is that Mom?

I must have dozed off as it seemed I began to daydream or was I in a trance? *What caused me to hear mom, even though my Ice Plant Ink had dried up? Oh no, my anxiety is kicking up again. Wait, is that it? No, no, it can't be. Could my eagerness to solve a problem or my anxiety and fear help me to daydream into my world? Hmm, let me focus harder and try to see mom.*

Although I didn't have any more Ice Plant Ink, I could "see" into my world where my father and mother were and I could hear them. I needed a target to focus on and I tried again.

Since I found Mom's car, that would be my target. With closed eyes, I imagined myself near Mom's car, and after a few moments, I could see the journal on the seat again and tried to open it to write another message.

"Why can't I manage to write a message this time? I am near Mom's car?" I questioned myself in a whisper.

Instantly, my mom's head turned as she heard her name. My dad had made it there. She invited him inside the cafe, they sat down to talk. I needed to hear them so I positioned myself on the ledge, just outside of the cafe, I could hear.

"Jake, why on earth are you planning to marry that woman? She's evil and tried to get me killed? She sent me to a church which was some kind of detour if you ask me. I found flying gargoyles and books that flew and attacked me. I nearly crashed driving out of there so fast," my mom told my dad.

My dad responded, "I never expected to experience any-thing like this. You know I went with Josh and Leilani to a castle? I was carried by those winged creatures and nearly died too!"

I continued to listen as my dad told my mom all about his adventures. As I listened, my interest was piqued when I heard about the Shaman in the hospital. I knew of him, but I wasn't sure of the whole story. It appeared that neither one of my parents knew exactly who this person was, however, my dad revealed something important!

"I met the Shaman, and he told me to get my journal, that there was some type of hidden message inside, which seemed strange to me since I authored it. He also began to cry profusely and trapped his tears inside this vile. I'm supposed to give these to Joshua, he said to help him fight off anyone that tries to harm him," Dad said to my mom.

My mom and dad continued to talk, but my mind was distracted. I urgently needed to figure out a way to get those tears.

Just then I was interrupted by Selia; she had my spear and map in hand.

"Joshua, go see your parents. It's brief, but necessary," she said, handing me the map and spear.

"Selia, you are truly a genius, I have known since we began this venture that you have saved my life!" I said to Selia as I began to draw the station, my mom's car and then moved toward it.

"Joshua, you only have a few minutes. This isn't supposed to let you stay long, just hurry," I heard Selia say as I departed into the picture on the map.

"Mom! Dad! I miss you so much!" I said to them both.

They looked at me, mom more astonished than dad, but both happy to see me.

"Oh honey, I miss you and we are all trying to help. Can't you just come home now?" my mom asked.

"Mom, I have to help, that's the only way I can come home for good. I only have a few minutes, but I heard you and dad talking. Dad what's this about tears?"

"The old Shaman gave them to me, well his spirit did. I think he was actually dead and his ghost appeared."

"Where are they? I'm going to need them. I probably need them to fight and beat Gonthragon. Dad, you need to get your journal. There's a hidden message there, I have heard that the Shaman's Ice Plant Ink is the secret to controlling all worlds too. I need more of that, my spear, and these tears.

"We don't have the journal yet. It's with Kate," mom said.

"I know I can defeat Gonthragon. Dad, you and mom have to get your journal before Gonthragon gets hold of it. I think Kate is going to give it to him. Her house and the church have the same evil gargoyles that chased me and carried dad, Leilani, and me into his castle. She's working with him," I told them both.

"Joshua," my dad said, "We will get the journal. You be careful son. It's your destiny to save our world. I know what you saw and nobody must know any more than you've told us now. You are risking everything coming here, so go back and win!" my dad urged me with his comforting and supportive words.

I took the tears and made it back to find Selia, she handed me an old bottle labeled Ice Plant Ink.

"I told you I've come to help out. I know you need this to help you on your adventure, but now it's time for me to go. I've broken my honor letting you go back to your family, I'm afraid I'm of no use to you any more."

"Wait, no, Selia, I need you. You're my guide and truly have helped me," I pleaded.

"You truly are a hero and you can do this on your own. Joshua, I have faith, you must believe in yourself and go after Gonthragon. There is nobody else that can do what you're destined to do. Be safe, remember your tools, and most of all I wish you good luck," Selia said to me.

"Selia, am I ever going to see you again? You've helped me in so many ways, each and every time I've been stuck, you've helped me on my journey, what am I going to do without you? I cannot do this on my own," I sadly replied.

But before I could utter another word or drop another tear, she was gone, just as quickly as she appeared to help me.

I stood with my satchel, packed with my tools, Ice Plant Ink and the tears of the Shaman.

CHAPTER

Jake and Noel decided to take the path together, all the while they talked about their plan and told stories of their favorite family moments.

"I hope Leilani is safe," Noel said to Jake. "Do you think she is?"

"Leilani has the strength of two men. She's strong and was left in reliable hands. Snoob is taking care of her," said Jake.

Jake tried to reassure mom that Lelani was safe, but he could not escape the feelings or thoughts of the journey he'd been on over the past two days.

"I know you don't understand what's going on, but I guess it's time I tell you." Jake tried to prepare her for the news he had never before told her.

"Oh no, what?" Noel said as she stopped and turned to look at him while unlocking the car. They both entered and Jake continued.

"Long before we got married and had kids, and all the while before Josh had his eye surgery, I used to dream about faraway lands. I always heard the same voice too and the voice in my head was that of the Shaman whom I met yesterday," Jake explained.

"Really? I never knew!" Noel said.

"The dreams were so real, but then the dreams stopped as soon as Josh had his surgery. I thought nothing of it, until I began to experience his dreams without dreaming. Noel, I actually traveled to the castle of Gonthragon and was carried there by his gargoyles. I met the Shaman on my journey to find out more about Josh's eye and when I met him at the Masonic Homes, he gave me his tears and information about my journal. He vanished into thin air, just like magic."

"I have felt weird things lately and Kate and those gargoyles, ugh!" Noel responded.

"You know it to be true with all the things you've been experiencing lately. I'm afraid it must be about the prophecy my grandfather told me about when I was young," Jake revealed all this to her for the first time.

"Jake, why the heck have you not mentioned this prophecy to us, to me, before? Don't you think it's relevant?" Noel questioned Jake.

"I really did not think any of it was real, I mean would you?" Jake asked honestly.

"Well, no I guess not," Noel responded.

Silence fell between the two of them and as they peered off through the window of the car into the horizon where the sun rises. They could see smoke floating into the sky, trees cascading upon one another, houses on fire, and not a creature could be seen in the sky, which seemed to have absorbed all the smoke and reformed it into gray clouds.

"I sure hope he's okay," muttered Noel, breaking the silence.

"Me too," Jake replied.

Mysteriously, the car began to pick up speed as if it were possessed and exited from the freeway.

"Buckle up," Noel warned. "You never know what could happen. I've experienced strange things here today and seen things I actually believe you've dreamt about."

Both were on the ready and prepared as they drove down the narrow road leading to Jake's new home. As they drove down the long driveway, they didn't see any sign of visitors or others on the road and nothing noticeable as a sign of anything weird happening. Jake and Noel exited the car after parking at the edge of the tree Noel left earlier. The both walked the twenty feet toward the front door. Unfortunately, Jake did not have his keys, so they had to knock and used the heavy gargoyle knocker.

Kate answered and as soon as she opened the door responded to Jake, "Oh my silly, you don't have your keys," but her face turned angry when she saw Noel.

"What is she doing here?" Kate grilled Jake.

"Oh, well we were both out searching for Joshua and we ran into each other, isn't that a coincidence? I've come only for my journal. I know it's here. Have you seen it? Noel said you had it earlier, but she didn't get a chance to get it from you." Jake asked Kate.

Kate turned and handed a journal to Jake, "Is this really why you're here and not to come home? I've missed you darling."

"Kate, I'm searching for my son, and I need my journal to help find him. Now hand it over," Jake insisted of Kate.

"Here," she said, thrusting the journal into his hands. "Now get rid of her before you come back!" Kate ordered Jake.

As he looked through the pages of the journal, he noticed that all the entries were done with a single color pen and that days were entered, but dates were missing. He knew this wasn't his journal, but he also knew this probably wasn't the time to make a big scene.

"So what else do you need? If nothing, then you may leave Noel," Kate insisted.

"She's not leaving. We are searching for our son together. You see, Kate, I believe you know something that you aren't telling me, and Noel found a few strange things happening here when she was here earlier today. What can you tell me about that?" Jake asked.

"She did? Well, I'm not sure what she could be talking about. She and I had a little girly chat and then she left, that was about all," Kate said smirking at Noel.

"Oh, is that right? You didn't send her out to a church for my journal, telling her it was in the lost and found, yet you find it here? By the way, I know that isn't my journal, and I should know, so come on, Kate, hand over the real thing!" Jake insisted.

Just then she vaporized before their eyes, and gargoyles encircled their heads. They had to duck and run to avoid being snatched. It was a long distance with gargoyles chasing them, just to get the journal, but they needed it to communicate. Jake grabbed Noel's hand and they dodged gargoyles by weaving in and out of doorways. They headed out the front door, but a gargoyle reached down with its talons and tried to carry Noel away. Jake grabbed her legs, pulled, and she was freed.

"Are you okay?" Jake asked.

"No, but get to the car!" screamed Noel.

Jake grabbed Joshua's journal off the seat of the car and then headed for the tree.

Several gargoyles chased them now and there wasn't a soul in sight. Taking the fake journal and Joshua's journal Jake thought to smack them together around the base of the tree, something similar to what he did in his dreams as a kid, but nothing happened.

"Well, it was worth a try," Jake said.

"Okay, now what?" Noel asked.

"Run. We have to get into the forest. There's a pipe there where we can hide inside. They cannot get inside, they're too big. It leads underground," Jake urged and directed Noel.

Safe inside the pipe and underground, they checked out their wounds. Noel was bleeding on her forearm and shoulder. Jake took off his outer shirt and bandaged it.

"How does that feel?" he asked.

"Thanks, but it burns like hell!" Noel responded.

Noel proceeded to examine the journals. She turned page after page.

"How do you know this one is a fake?" Noel asked.

"I used different ink each time I wrote an entry. This one is the same ink throughout," Jake responded.

"How did you get out of that world and into this one?" Noel asked.

"I think it was the one that traveled with Joshua on his journey, Selia? She magically sent me directly to the hospital. I was also taken to the playground where we used to play with the kids, the Pepsi Park, but then when we all touched, we were transported to an open grasslands area, which was just before the gargoyles took us. I'm really not quite sure how we traveled, but I know Joshua has some type of power there or ability we don't," Jake said as he told as much about what he remembered as he could.

"Well, I don't think we should stay here all night. Kate's up to something. She probably is working with Gonthragon," Noel insisted.

"I agree. We do need to stay here a while though. Those gargoyles are persistent creatures and they'll be waiting a while," Jake said to her as he slouched to get comfortable.

Noel also adjusted herself inside the pipe. Both dozed off as Joshua's book flew open.

CHAPTER

om, dad, you're both safe…but it's no time to be sleeping on the job! Dad, you know I need that journal, ugh!

Great, I needed dad's journal. Selia told me I could not go back. Mom and dad slept and I had no idea if Leilani was doing all right or not.

Hhm, I wondered. Dad said he didn't know the secret of his journal. Could the tears and ink help unveil that?

I checked my map and used my pen. "Let's see, where is it I must go now?" I asked the map as I sat on the edge of a rock.

My pen slowly revealed the next phase of my journey to me, but I couldn't decipher what the image was…I squinted… *it looked like a Thragon!* Oh my, it was and clasped in its claws was a book! *I bet that's dad's journal!* The area surrounding the flying Thragon was engulfed in flames and I predicted his next move. I must take action.

I imagined myself on the edge of those talons and just as the vision was clear in my mind. *Whoosh*, I transported.

The Thragon held the book tight and shot fire on me. I dodged it and reached for the book, took hold, and pulled, ugh…but the grasp was too tight. *Think Josh! Oh yeah, I have good old fire-starter. Let me heat up those talons!* I reached into my satchel, pulled out the fire-starter and flicked it onto the gargoyle's leg. Just as I did this, the book fell from its grasp. I also started to fall, but thankfully I had my hiking boots and my whip, I grabbed the book, swung the whip around the Thragon's neck and instantly it transformed into a beautiful flying bird! Its neck was long and covered in beautiful purple fur. I looked down. I sat on a silver saddle with smoothed out ridges, perhaps where a royal crown had been molded. The gargoyle was friendly, no longer a Thragon, and the struggle was no longer an issue. We flew to a distant edge of Gonthragon's castle! I tied up my new friend, just in case I needed a quick escape! I took the book and my tools and began my search for Leilani. I traveled through corridors, tried to remember the path of the secret doors. I successfully found my way into the room where we met Snoob!

Odd, no guards? Why weren't gargoyles trying to attack me?

Strangely, there seemed to be no guards or gargoyles and I hadn't been spotted by anyone or thing!

I wondered, was he here? I approached the entrance to his throne and was met by Leilani! What are you doing here?

"I've been trying to find a way out, but each time those gargoyles find me. I thought I'd try to find out more about Gonthragon to take him down, but there's nothing but his orb post left. Isn't that strange? You would think that would stay behind, right?" Leilani exclaimed!

"Well, I think the orb is his actual eye! He says he needs me to look into his orb and when I stared into it before, he became enraged! He saw what I did and into the worlds where I went and was able to penetrate them! I don't recall seeing his face during that moment. His eye must have been the orb! I need to find him, get the journal, and then I can end his destruction!" I informed Leilani, but no sooner had the words left my mouth a swoosh and swoop came and lifted me up, Snoob rushed to protect Leilani, but it was too late, both of us were in flight and Gonthragon breathed a torrent of flames toward Snoob.

"Nooooo!" we screamed in unision, tears flowing down our cheeks. I don't think he survived.

We were taken to the place where it all began, the land of the Norkels, near Green Burroughs Valley and into the Ice Plants I fell! Again!

"Run, go hide in the Ice Plant slides, they will protect you!" I yelled to Leilani.

Gonthragon swooped to the ground, scratching toward me with his talons and shot flames of fire to burn me. I was faster. I had my hiking boots on. The speed and my pen kept me alive. *My pen?* It appeared to be thwarting the flames! I was amazed. I examined it closer, clicked it, and it became a shield!

"Eat your heart out Captain America," I yelled, excited to be defending myself with an equitably heroic device!

I tried to get myself into a corner to ascertain what secrets were in my dad's journal, but Gonthragon kept me busy.

"I'll throw Ice Plant flowers at him to distract him, hurry Josh!" Leilani yelled.

"Don't let him get you. He'll kill you! Leilani!" I yelled back.

The first concoction I made was mixed tears and Ice Plant ink and put that on the end of the spear. Nothing! *Okay?*

Gonthragon soared toward me, but I jumped out of his way and onto the Ice Plant slide near Leilani. He smashed to the ground.

"The journal?" she said. "You have to hurry!"

"I know!" I'm looking through it. I don't see anything secret," I said.

But Gonthragon wasn't finished with me yet. Back at it, he grabbed my hand with his talon, I almost lost the tears, but nothing spilled out!

"That was too close! Don't get near him!" she demanded.

"I'd like to see you try to do this!" I yelled.

Angry at both of them, I grabbed my shield and tried to stop Gonthragon. He was relentless as he threw flames and lashed out with his talons! I dodged them!

"My shield is helping, but I need more help or weapons!" I screamed.

"You are the one, the only one. Remember the prophecy?" she reminded me.

Think, Josh, my *spirit sticks! Oh yeah!*

Turning around his large body took time, enough so I could run over to the carriage. The sticks glowed at my arrival, although not really sure how to use them, I grabbed them. Gonthragon was in for it and I wasn't going down, not today! I approached, not knowing what to do with them, but Gonthragon backed off! Just like magic! *Hhm, what the heck? Well...good, but this can't last long.* Now, let me get back to the book...and as I turned the last page, the back lining tore a bit and revealed these words:

> To defeat the ogre, you must mix Ice Plant ink, tears of the Shaman, and its blood with the charmed pen, sprinkled with Sacred Tea leaves. Dab this in the one severed the Shaman, and stare into its eye!

What in the world does that mean?

"Leilani, I think I found it!" I said.

"I knew it. What exactly did you find?" she asked.

"Words, I think...well, it could be how to defeat him, but I'm not sure what it means," I said. "Can you help?"

"Okay, calm down, read it to me," she said.

"To defeat the ogre you must mix ice plant ink, tears of the Shaman and its blood. That's the first part," I said. I have Ice Plant Ink and can get more while I'm here or from inside my pen where I found the scroll. "

"True. Dad just gave you the tears," she replied.

"And you and Selia got the Sacred Tea Leaves in your satchel, right?" she asked.

"We've used some, but I hope I have a few more!" I said.

"Its blood? Who is it?" she asked.

"Oh my God, well…I presume it's Gonthragon!" I said, worried about how to get that.

"Wait, how—?" but Leilani was cut off by me.

"How am I going to get his blood?" I asked.

She ducked back behind the Ice Plants, Gonthragon made noises of an approach again.

Okay, well, I have a charmed pen, that's always helpful and because I'm destined to be the hero, it must be my pen they are referring to, after all, I was told it's "charmed!" Now, this last part, I'm not sure what that means! Dab this in the one severed the Shaman and stare into its eye!

Out of nowhere, Gonthragon clawed my arm, grabbed my spear, ink, map, and before he could get out of sight, I scratched at his talon, which produced a small amount of blood!

"Gonthragon may have taken my map, but I had the pen, though he could use the ink to travel almost anywhere, especially other worlds!" I said to Leilani.

"Great! We just need to get out of here!" we said together and as we both thought of ways to get out, destruction ensues.

Gonthragon flew away. I presumed he thought he won, but my eye revealed something. Call it a spiritual connection, premonition, but given the totality of all it's helped me do, I watched.

He's burned almost all of the Norkels' lands, all of Green Burroughs Valley, and the Ice plants began and continued to burn before our eyes.

He must be miffed I still had the journal and Ice Plant slides secret and could stop him. Our next meeting would be his end. He knew that.

"Gonthragon knows my weakness. He's burning Hayward, this world and all neighborhoods. He must be destroyed," I said to Leilani, but to myself too.

I closed my eyes and could see more, much more! My eye revealed several towns, schools, houses, roads, bridges… burned, just like my vision in the orb!

"Selia! Selia! You always told me you would be there. Where are you? I need you, my home, my friends, the inhabitants of this region, all are burning! Please help!

Leilani came to my side and hugged me.

"Selia, I care for all these creatures in your world and mine! We must overpower the evil of Gonthragon!" I begged of Selia, but it seemed to no avail!

Jake and Noel woke up. Most of the forest they were in burned and smoke entered the pipe.

"Jake, I have Joshua's journal. Maybe we can get a message to him somehow?" said Noel.

But Josh and Leilani were three steps ahead of them!

CHAPTER

"That's great! I have all I need, except we are now trapped here and Gonthragon is destroying everything!" I said irritatingly to anyone who would listen besides Leilani. But she was the only one that heard me.

"How do we get out of here now?" she asked.

"I don't know!" I replied.

"Where's the journal?" Leilani asked me?

"I have it, but the purpose of getting it was to reveal how to stop...'*how to stop Gonthragon!*' *The Journal?* Leilani, you are brilliant! Mom has MY journal and I forgot, I can control it with my charmed pen and my eye!" I informed Leilani.

"What? So then let's send a message!" she exclaimed.

"Okay, so let me think. We need them to know we are trapped and—" I said.

"That they need to get help or get the map back!" she continued.

"Okay, I'll say that!" I said.

Mom and Dad,

Leilani and I are stuck here in the Ice plants. We need the map. Gonthragon took it. If you can get a message to someone to get to us, great! Ice plants are burning! Gonthragon has destroyed everything! I have what I needed from the journal, but I need family and friends to support me in this. Please help!

Love,

Josh and Leilani

Noel rolled over in the pipe. She had heard a crinkle sound and briefly looked to see what it was that woke her up. Surprised, she saw the message as it was being written in Josh's journal! She could hardly contain herself, as she pushed Jake over to wake him up,

"Look!" she said.

"What, I'm sleeping." Jake responded rolling back over.

"Jake! Josh, Leilani, Gonthragon!…The journal!" Noel screamed at Jake.

Jake turned and read the words, just as they ended.

"Josh, journal…w-w-what?"

"Jake!" Noel said, pushing him out of the pipe.

"Noel, what are you doing?" he asked, coughing from smoke inhalation.

She showed him the journal again. He took a minute, but then responded.

"Oh Josh, I knew you could do it, always thinking on your toes and fighting off the bad guys! We need to get to Soran or Pergita! Quickly!" Jake told Noel.

"Who are they?" She questioned.

"We met them briefly and I know if Josh is this close to defeating Gonthragon, they can help!" he advised.

Back at home, Hayward news reported of major destruction of large flying creatures. Speculations of aliens were all over the broadcast news! Bridges, coastlands, all being burned down.

Noel stood at the edge of the pipe. Jake handed her the Tea leaves from the tree she mentioned. The one Joshua told her about earlier and the one she found as she followed them.

Selia stood listening to the tea leaves, but not sure of the message.

"What is this? It must be Joshua's mom. She's in a pipe. She's with Jake, but what's this? Oh no, I must go and contact everyone!" Selia said as impact of the message finally struck her.

Noel succeeded in reaching Selia. It had been planned by Selia a while back, when she was in the forest with Joshua, that once he needed help and was on his path to destroying Gonthragon, his friends and family, those that knew how and what to do, could use the tea leaves. Selia successfully contacted Noel and her plan was triumphant! Even though she had broken the rules once before, Josh ultimately reached the necessary point on his journey. She had set the team in motion. She had more power than previously thought.

Soran arrived with his team of Norkel soldiers, Wormly brought the carriage, which had newly installed flying wheels! Selia brought the flying goose and picked up Jake and Noel.

Everyone prepared to help Josh defeat Gonthragon.

Hearing of this assembly, Gonthragon brought out the Thragons and headed to the land of the Ice Plants.

"Hey…how? Where? Oh, never mind. I'm glad you're here," I said to Soran.

Selia approached me. I hugged her.

"Selia, I thought you left me for good! I'm glad you're here now. I—" she cut me off.

"I know what you've been through and we are here, it's the prophecy in action. You must fight and we are here to help where we can," she advised me.

Gonthragon swooped in, just as she uttered the last word. I was ready and everyone watched.

Mom and dad were huddled with Leilani as this was my battle to fight alone! My comrades, Soran, Selia, Wormly, Pergita, and all others in this story are at the ready, there to support me!

"Now, all I need to do is get near his eye, I have the mixture of *ice plant ink, Shaman tears, Gonthragon's blood, stirred with my pen, sprinkled with Sacred Tea leaves and dabbed in my eye. All I need to do is stare into his eye!" Josh* bragged.

Gargoyles, several of them, approached me as I ran toward Wormly, pushed him out of the carriage and began to fly around!

"Whoohoo! I love the newly improved carriage! Thanks, Wormly!" I yelled as the gargoyles attack.

Impenetrable by their talons, they shoot fire at me, but I'm immune to their attacks!

"Those are the Thragons turned gargoyle!" Soran hollered.

We go round and round and my carriage, spear, whip and pen were perfect weapons against the gargoyles. Thragons that turned into gargoyles, weren't that bad, now that I had protection! *I only wish I had this before my journey began.*

Gonthragon noticed his new army of gargoyles weren't causing damage and traveled my way.

How am I going to get to his eye? Once I do, I can end him! If I can get my carriage to fly close enough, I can jump on his back and straddle his wings long enough to stare him down. This was my plan!

Seconds turn into minutes, but finally he approached. He had my map and seemed to enter and exit at will and never completed any particular flight pattern. *My map! He can appear and disappear! Ugh!* I had forgotten he had my map. This would be more difficult than I had previously thought!

Gonthragon flew directly over my head, then disappeared and then reappeared behind me! I tried to get close, but he escaped too quickly! *My weapons! Will my pen work, even though he has control over it? I'm sure, it's meant to only work for me! Most others with powers can only disappear and reappear within seconds...whereas I can disappear longer. Hhmm... well, it's worth a try!* My plan, I would disappear and reappear directly in front of him.

Gonthragon just disappeared...and when he reappears, I'll make my move!

"Go," I said aloud, and I disappeared with pen in hand!

Gonthragon looked confused. He slowed down, looked around, and seemed frozen still. This was my turn. I held his gaze, my eye directly in front of his, dabbed more mixture for good measure, then reappeared and landed on his head! Gonthragon, angered, turned his head from side to side and attempted to throw me off. He avoided my eye. I stared straight, ready for him when he turned to face me with his orbed eye!

But when he did, his eye was gone! *What? OMG, he left it back at his castle, he knows I know! I need it!*

I grabbed the map from him and disappeared!

Quickly I sent another message to my mom and dad and used my map to find the orbed eye!

The orbed eye must be at the castle. It wasn't in Gonthragon's eye socket. Tell everyone! I wrote to mom. *I'm going to find it.*

Gonthragon had the ink and had been able to see into my world and mind for a while. I'm sure he knew he had power to escape to other worlds and realms. If he was not guarding his orbed eye, then he escaped!

The castle was dark and I smelt the flesh of burnt gargoyles! Weird sensations vanquished, which was a great sign. I needed to stare into the orb. Gonthragon would be stopped and lands would heal!

As I approached the orb, I awaited danger and approached slowly, but no danger appeared! My heart was relieved. The orb had been cracked and I wasn't sure this would work. I tried anyway. As I stared into the orb, my eye began to swirl, both eyes hovered above my head, spun around and clicked together! My eye returned to my socket, the other to the orbed post, and as I stared at it, the crack repaired! I took a moment, looked into the orb again and what I saw was familiar!

The earliest Christmas I could remember, mom, dad, and my grandparents were there. I hadn't seen them for a while, but I was only two! My grandpa came over to me, gave me a pen, map, and magical marble! He told me to keep an eye on it and winked! *That was it!* In that moment, as I stared at my memory, I knew who Gonthragon was and where he went! I would catch him someday!

Selia appeared instantly.

"Joshua your journey has only begun. You think you've discovered the true identity of Gonthragon and what happened so very long ago, but that's only the beginning," she said and gave me a hug before returning us all to the land of the Ice Plants.

24

CHAPTER

Upon my return to the land of the Ice Plants, I was reminded that we needed the Ancient Sacred Tea leaves to return to Hayward and the love of family and friends!

Soran approached me and said, "We thank you for saving both our worlds! I'm not sure what happened, but I can guess you defeated Gonthragon?"

"Well, sort of," I said.

"I knew you would! Please take this token of appreciation," he said and handed me the pen and map. "You never know when you'll need them!"

"Wow, cool! Thanks, Soran!"

"We also want to invite you back anytime. You've unlocked the path between our worlds now with your bravery and love! Your heart is strong and we are indebted to you!" he said.

"I don't know what to say. I really missed my family and was ready to give up when I first met you Soran, and you Wormly," I said.

"You are a hero," Wormly said slithering alongside me once more.

"Gonthragon escaped, you should know this. I think I know where, but as long as he's gone and I can get back home, we should be happy, right?" I said shrugging my shoulders.

"The invitation is there. Use it if you like," Soran and Wormly said as the inhabitants all begin to scatter and go back to normal daily routines.

We all hugged, I left my tools with the exception of the gifts and my family and I traveled home!

The portal, which was once again opened, led us to the spot where my journey into the land of the Ice Plants began. We all just stood on the sidewalk at the edge of the Ice Plants, shaking our heads!

"I can't believe this is where it all started!" I said.

"I know you all have worked up an appetite, so let's head over to Chipotle to celebrate our family, Josh's bravery and… oh, I don't know…LIFE!" my mom said.

We all sighed, laughed, and agreed.

"Jada and Jonah, are they meeting us there?" I asked Mom.

"Let's swing by the house and pick them up!" she said.

We all drove off to dinner at Chipotle, reminisced about the day, family, and I told them what I encountered when I found the orbed-eye. *Family is what you make of it.*

The next day I headed out with mom for the first day of school at my new school and we got a phone call. The mayor of Hayward, Barbara Halliday, wanted to give my family the *key to the city* for saving ours and many towns. She invited us to a dinner and a celebration that evening.

"Wow, the key to the city? You are truly a hero Josh!" my mom said.

"Thanks mom! I only did it because I love you all and I couldn't get back home until I helped out!" I told them all.

When I finally made it to school, my new teacher and peers had found out what happened. They made me "kid of the year" even though I just started the school!

"We are so proud of your efforts, Joshua! It's amazing, especially given the reasons you were sent here!" Ms. Michelle acknowledged me.

"I'm happy to be here too. I only wish every kid could feel how I do at this moment! I hope my friends can experience happiness, bravery, fear, and all that I did. I believe we are all heroes!" I said to her and everyone in group.

My day went quickly and I took the bus home. When I opened the door, I noticed I had a letter waiting for me. It was from an anonymous author and had no return address or markings of any kind. I opened it, half-reluctant and half-excited.

Dear Josh,

You have just begun your journeys. Now you've proven yourself worthy. It's your destiny to be a hero, to solve mysteries, save worlds, and to make a difference. Your place is between both of the worlds in which your latest journeys have taken you and yours with your American family! Have you wondered why you imagine, dream, and are unlike anyone else? Your true identity and that of your family will be revealed in time.

Enjoy the quiet. It won't last long!

It won't last long? What? Before my journey, I hated my life, then after I became a hero, I had been surprisingly happy, so different from what I felt before my adventures! *Now this letter! What does it mean? I'm not done fighting in other worlds? I'm not who I think I am, neither is my family? What?*

"Josh, are you home? Did you get the mail?" my mom questioned.

I had not gotten the mail. In fact, this letter and others were on the table when I got home. Just as I said that, the letter in my hand disappeared into thin air! And if this had happened before my latest adventures, I would have freaked out. But now, today...I'm used to strange things, and letters that disappeared were no longer alarming!

ABOUT THE AUTHOR

 Dawnette N. Brenner is a sixth-grade teacher as well as a mother of four adult children and grandmother of three. She's been teaching for thirteen years and was raised in the San Francisco Bay Area, currently living in the California Central Valley. She's an avid reader and enjoys mystery, fantasy, and CSI stories. In her spare time, she enjoys teaching kids to code and has created a Makerspace with a 3-D printer in the past. Currently, she runs both robotics and coding clubs. She's working on book 2 in this series. Stay tuned.

CPSIA information can be obtained
at www.ICGtesting.com
Printed in the USA
LVOW03s0705301017
554271LV00001B/250/P